COUNTRY LEGACY

COUNTRY
LEGACY

THE MAVERICK'S CHRISTMAS BABY

USA TODAY BESTSELLING AUTHOR

Victoria Pade

Special thanks and acknowledgment are given to
Victoria Pade for her contribution to the
Montana Mavericks: Rust Creek Cowboys continuity.

PLEASE RECYCLE
THIS PRODUCT IS RECYCLABLE

Recycling programs
for this product may
not exist in your area.

ISBN-13: 978-1-335-52357-0

The Maverick's Christmas Baby
First published in 2013. This edition published in 2022.
Copyright © 2013 by Harlequin Enterprises ULC

For questions and comments about the quality of this book,
please contact us at CustomerService@Harlequin.com.

Harlequin Enterprises ULC
22 Adelaide St. West, 41st Floor
Toronto, Ontario M5H 4E3, Canada
www.Harlequin.com

Printed in U.S.A.

Victoria Pade is a *USA TODAY* bestselling author of numerous romance novels. She has two beautiful and talented daughters—Cori and Erin—and is a native of Colorado, where she lives and writes. A devoted chocolate lover, she's in search of the perfect chocolate-chip-cookie recipe.

For information about her latest and upcoming releases, visit Victoria Pade on Facebook—she would love to hear from you.

Chapter 1

"Oh, this is not good…" Nina Crawford said to herself as she cautiously pulled her SUV to a stop at the sign on the isolated country road outside her hometown.

Mother Nature had not been kind to Rust Creek Falls this year. First a summer flood had devastated the small Montana town, and now—still in the midst of trying to recover from that—it was being hit by a December blizzard.

The weather report had predicted only a moderate storm that would arrive later tonight. Nina ran her family's general store in town and, trusting that weather report, when an elderly, arthritic customer on an outlying farm had called in and asked that a heating pad be delivered to her, Nina hadn't hesitated to leave the store in the hands of her staff and grant that request. And even when that lonely elderly woman had offered Christmas cookies and chamomile tea, Nina still hadn't had any worries about spending an hour visiting.

But the sky had grown increasingly ominous and dark with storm clouds, and when the first few flakes began to fall much earlier than they were supposed to, Nina had left.

Only to find herself miles from home when the howling winds had whipped that snow into a blinding frenzy.

Temperatures had plummeted rapidly, and already the snow was freezing to the windows of Nina's SUV, adding to the limitations of her vision. She rolled down her window, hoping to be able to better see if another vehicle was coming from her left.

It didn't help much. Visibility was low. Very, very low.

She studied the crossroads, searching for anything that might give her an indication that another car was coming. But she didn't see any approaching headlights in the whiteout conditions, and all she could hear was the screaming wind. So, hoping the coast was clear, she rolled up her window and ventured into her right turn.

But the moment she got out onto the road she did see headlights. Coming straight for her.

Trying to avoid a collision she swerved sharply, and so did the other vehicle.

The next thing Nina knew her SUV was nose-down in a ditch and she'd fallen pregnant-belly-first into the steering wheel.

Which was when she felt the first pain.

"No, no, no, no…"

Fighting the rise of panic, she did what she could to push herself back from the steering wheel—which at that angle was no easy task.

Her due date was January 13. It was currently two weeks before Christmas. If her baby was born now it would be a month early.

She *couldn't* deliver a month early.

She couldn't….

A pounding on her side window startled her and the fright didn't help matters.

"Are you all right?" a man's voice shouted in to her.

Her SUV hadn't hit anything so her airbag hadn't activated and the engine was still running. But dazed and scared, she didn't know if she was all right. She just couldn't think straight.

Then the door was opened from the outside. And standing there was Dallas Traub!

It wasn't exactly encouraging to see a member of the family that had been at odds with her own for generations.

"Are you all right?" he repeated.

"I don't know. I may be going into labor. I think I need help...."

"Okay, stay calm. My truck is stuck, too, on the other side of the road. But at least it isn't nearly up on end the way you are. If we can get you out of here you can lie down in my backseat."

Fear and the dull ache in her abdomen robbed Nina of the ability to argue. Traub or not, he was all there was and she was going to have to accept his aid.

"Can you turn off the engine?" he asked.

That made sense but it hadn't occurred to Nina. And, yes, she could do that, so she did, leaving the keys in the ignition.

"I'm glad to see that you can move your arms. Do you have feeling everywhere— arms, legs, hands, feet?"

"Yes."

"Did you hit your head? Do you have any neck pain?"

"No, I didn't hit my head and I don't have any neck pain. I just hit the steering wheel."

"Are you bleeding from anywhere? Did your water break?"

As odd as it seemed, not even a question that personal sounded out of place at that point.

"I don't think I'm bleeding, no. And I'm perfectly dry...."

"Good. All good," he judged. "Would it be okay if I lifted you out of there?"

"I think so...."

"Let me do all the work," he advised. Sliding one arm under her legs, the other behind her back, he gently but forcefully pulled her toward him until she found herself extracted from behind the wheel and cradled against his big, masculine chest.

"Maybe I can walk...." Nina said.

"We're not going to take any chances," he responded, wasting no time heading across the road.

The man was dressed in a heavy fleece-lined suede jacket, but Nina had to assume that he was all muscle underneath it because he carried her as if she weighed nothing.

And when he reached the white truck that was nearly invisible in the snow blowing all around it, he even managed to open the rear door on the double cab.

Another cramp struck Nina as he eased her onto the backseat and her panic must have been obvious to him because he said, "It's okay. Just breathe through it. It'll pass and we'll get someone out here before you know it."

"And if my baby doesn't wait for that?" Nina nearly shouted over the wind.

"I've been in a delivery room for three of my own kids and birthed more animals than I can count—if it comes to that, I can take care of it. We'll be fine."

It crossed her mind to call him a liar because nothing about this was at all fine. But there was actually something soothing in his composure, in his take-charge attitude, and Traub or not, Nina had to hope that he really could get her through this if need be.

Just please don't let there be the need....

"We should conserve fuel, so I'll turn on the engine long enough to get it warm in here, then we'll turn it off again," he explained, closing the rear door and getting into the front of the cab from the passenger seat to slide across and turn the key in the ignition. "But I'm going to leave my hazards flashing, to make sure anyone approaching can see us in the snow."

Warm air instantly drifted back to Nina but she was feeling more uncomfortable lying down, and she pushed herself to sit up to see if that helped.

It actually did and she explained that. "Just see if you can get someone out here to us," she instructed.

That was when he tried his cell phone and found that he had no reception.

"Try mine," Nina said, taking it out of the pocket of her wool winter coat to hand to him, fighting renewed panic.

But her phone was as useless as his was.

"Oh, God..." Nina lamented as every muscle in her body tensed.

"Another contraction?" he asked.

"No, I don't think so," she answered, so scared she wasn't sure what she was feeling beyond that.

He angled sideways in the front seat. "We're gonna be fine. I promise," he said in a way that made her believe it and relax a little again.

Until he said, "There are pockets out here

where you can get cell reception if you just hit one. I'll walk out a ways and see if maybe—"

"No! You can't leave!" Nina said in full-out panic once again. "You know the stories about farmers getting lost in storms like this just trying to find their way between their house and barn. You can't go!"

"I do know the stories," he said.

Then he slid to the passenger side again and got out of the truck.

A moment later he climbed into the backseat with her, carrying a thick coil of rope she'd heard him drag out of the truck bed. He rolled down the rear passenger window, held one end of the rope and tossed the rest of the coil through the window. Then he rolled the window up again, catching the rope in a small gap at the top of it.

"Okay..." he said then, handing her the end of the rope that he'd retained. "Hang on to this, I'll hang on to the other end and I won't go any farther than the length of it. If you need me, just yank and I'll come right back. Otherwise, I'll use it to make sure I *can* get back."

"You'll be careful?"

"I will be. And I'll leave the engine running to keep you warm in the meantime. All right?"

"I suppose," Nina agreed reluctantly, holding on to that rope with a tight fist.

Dallas Traub wrapped his hand around hers and squeezed. "Everything is going to be okay," he said confidently.

Her own hand wasn't cold, and yet his around it felt even warmer. It was also slightly rough and callused, and the size and strength of it along with those signs of hard ranch work all infused her with more of a sense of calm and a renewed belief that he could and would take care of her. Traub or not. Regardless of what happened.

Nina even managed to smile weakly. "Be careful," she said, thinking of his safety, too.

"I will."

He let go of her hand and Nina was surprised to find herself sorry to lose his touch. Which was what she was thinking when he opened the door, ducked under the rope and got out, leaving her alone. And sorry to lose his company, too. His comforting presence.

The touch, the company, the presence of a Traub.

She closed her eyes and breathed deeply again, willing herself to settle down for the sake of her baby, willing her baby to rest, to stay put, not to be born today....

Then another cramp struck.

"Please, no, not yet," she begged her unborn child and the fates, as if that could stop things if she really was going into labor.

How long had Dallas Traub been gone? It seemed like forever and Nina looked across the front seat through the windshield, hoping to spot him. But all she could see was snow.

She caught sight of herself in the rearview mirror then and realized that the stocking cap she had on was askew. For some odd reason she regretted that Dallas had seen her looking so disheveled, so she straightened the cap. She also gave in to the urge to fluff her hair a bit where the long brown locks cascaded from beneath the cap past her shoulders.

Her ordinarily pink cheeks were quite pale and she reached up and pinched them to add some color. Her mascara had survived the accident and all that followed it without smudging beneath her very dark brown eyes, but unfortunately her thin, straight nose had a bit of a shine that she didn't like to see.

She tried to blot that with the back of her hand, regretting that she'd left her purse in her SUV with her compact in it. And with her lip gloss in it, too.

Not that, in the midst of possible peril, she

was actually thinking about putting on lipstick to accentuate lips she sometimes thought were not full enough. She merely wanted to moisten those lips to keep them from chapping, she told herself. Certainly it wasn't that she cared at all what she looked like at that moment. Especially to a Traub. When she'd just had a car accident. When she could potentially be going into labor.

But, oh, she wished this particular Traub would come back....

She considered yanking on the rope just to get him to, but she didn't let herself. They needed help and if there was any chance that he might find cell reception she couldn't cut that short.

But soon, come back soon....

Then, as if in answer to her silent plea, the rear passenger door opened and there he was.

She also didn't understand why the way he looked registered in that instant, but she was struck by how tall and capable-looking he was. She guessed him to be about six foot three inches of broad-shouldered, Western masculinity.

But it wasn't merely his size that impressed her. He was remarkably handsome—something else that she'd never noticed in all the times they must have crossed paths around Rust Creek Falls.

Nina knew all the Traubs in general, but she'd never really noted much about them in any kind of detail. Now it struck her that Dallas really did have rugged good looks with a squarish forehead, a nose that was a bit hooked, but in a dashing sort of way, lips that were full and almost lush, and striking blue eyes that had enough of a hint of gray to add more depth than she'd ever have attributed to a Traub.

"Did you get a call out?" she asked as he extracted the end of the rope through the window, tossed the re-coiled mass into the truck bed again and then climbed into the backseat with her, closing the door and the window after himself.

"No," he said. "We're really in a dead zone out here. But don't worry about it. Somebody will come looking for us. My folks are stuck at home with my three boys—believe me, before too long they'll start to wonder where I am." Then he switched gears and asked, "How are you doing?"

"I'm okay...." Nina answered uncertainly.

"Any more pains?"

"One," she admitted.

"And how about heat? Think we can turn it off for a little while?"

"Sure. If you're warm enough."

He stood to lean over the front seat to reach the key, and Nina found herself sneaking a glance at him from that angle.

He was wearing jeans that hugged an impressive derriere and thick thighs, and she knew she had no business taking note of any of that.

Then the engine went off and he sat back down, turning toward her and perching on the very edge of the seat so he could pull down the rear cushion as he said, "There should be a blanket in here…"

He produced a heavy plaid blanket from the compartment hidden behind the seat.

"You're probably not going to like this, but we'll both stay warmer if we share the blanket and some body heat," he said then.

"It's okay," Nina agreed, knowing he was right.

And not totally hating the idea of having him close beside her or of sharing the blanket with him. But she didn't analyze that.

Opening the heavy emergency blanket, he set it over Nina and reached across her to tuck it in on her other side.

Then he sat near enough to share the warmth he exuded and laid it across himself, too.

"You're sure you feel better sitting up?" he asked.

"I am."

"If something changes and you need to lie down just let me know…."

"I will," Nina said.

She did slump a little more into the blanket, though. And somehow that brought her a bit closer to him, too. But he didn't seem to mind that she was slightly tucked to his side and it seemed as though it might be insulting if she moved away again, so she pretended that she didn't notice.

"So…" he said when she was settled, turning his head toward her and looking down at her. "You're *Nina* Crawford, right? You run the General Store in town?"

Apparently Dallas Traub wasn't any clearer about the details of his Crawford rivals than Nina was about the Traubs. And since they'd never had any one-on-one, face-to-face contact before this, Nina was even surprised that he knew her name.

"I'm Nina, right. And yes, I run the store." The store that the Traubs rarely frequented, making it well-known that they chose to do their shopping in nearby Kalispell rather than give business to the Crawfords.

"I'm Dallas—in case you didn't know...."

"You live on your family's ranch—the Triple T, right?"

"I do work on the ranch, but I have my own house on the property. I'm divorced, and with three boys—Ryder, who's ten, Jake, eight, and Robbie, who just turned six a couple of weeks ago."

"And you have custody of them?" Nina asked, recalling that no one was too sure what had happened to his marriage, but that it had ended about this time last year. Gossip had been rampant and she remembered thinking that, since he was a Traub, his wife had probably just wised up. Nina hadn't found it so easy to understand why his ex-wife had left her kids behind, though.

Now, appreciating the way Dallas had been caring for her, appreciating the effort he was putting into distracting her by making conversation, how just plain kind and friendly he was being toward her, she had less understanding of his wife's leaving him, too.

"Yep, it's all me, all the time..." he said somewhat forlornly and without any of the confidence he'd shown in every other way since he'd opened her car door. "Not that my family isn't good about helping out—they are. But still—"

"You're the Number One in Charge. Of *three* kids."

"And there's nothing easy about being a single parent," he said, clearly feeling the weight of it. His gaze went for a split second in the direction of her middle. "I guess I don't know many specifics about the Crawfords," he said then. "I probably know the most about your brother Nate now, just from the election for mayor—"

"Since he was running against your brother Collin and lost," Nina pointed out.

"But I don't think I knew you were married or pregnant...."

"Pregnant, not married. Never have been."

"But you were with someone weren't you? Leo Steadler? He did some work for us a couple of years back and—"

"I was with Leo for four years." Four years that had led only to disappointment.

"But he left town, didn't he?"

Nina could hear the confusion and suspicions that were mounting. "He did."

"Rather than stepping up?"

There was outrage in that that made Nina smile. "The baby isn't Leo's."

"Oh."

She smiled again, having a pretty good idea what he was filling in the blanks with. The same things her own family had assumed—first that the baby was Leo's, then that she'd had some kind of rebound fling that had resulted in an unwanted pregnancy.

But they were all wrong. And since she wasn't ashamed of the choice she'd made and had been perfectly honest with everyone else, she decided to be perfectly honest now, even with Dallas Traub.

"After four wasted years with Leo, when it ended I decided I wasn't going to wait for another man to come along." And make more empty promises of *someday*. "There was no telling how long it might take to meet someone—"

"If ever," he muttered as if he held absolutely no optimism when it came to finding a soul mate.

"And then what?" Nina went on. "What if I used up another year or two or three or *four* and found myself right where I was after Leo? I'd just be older and I still wouldn't have the baby I've always wanted. The family. And sometimes you just have to go after what you want, regardless of what anyone else thinks. So I took some time off, went to a sperm bank in Denver without telling my family—"

"You just did that on your own?"

"I did," Nina said with all the conviction she'd felt then still in her voice. "I didn't see the point in sitting through people trying to talk me out of it, so I just did it. And, voilà! The magic of modern medicine—I'm having the baby I want, on my own."

Looking up at him, Nina watched him nod slowly, ruminatively, his well-shaped eyebrows arching over those gray-tinged blue eyes. "Wow," he said, as if he didn't quite know what to make of her. "My family is very big on marriage and would freak out over something like that. How did yours take it?"

"They freaked out," Nina confirmed. "But when the dust settled…" She shrugged. "I've always been my own person and strong-willed and…well, hard to stop once I put my mind to something. My family has just sort of gotten used to that. And a baby? That's a good thing. So after the initial shock, they got on board."

"I'd say *that* was a good thing, otherwise

having a baby on your own might be kind of an overwhelming proposition."

"But I just didn't want to wait anymore."

"You seem kind of young for the clock to be ticking loud enough to go that route."

"That was something my family said. I'm twenty-five, so sure, my age isn't an issue. Except that I've always wanted to have kids fairly young, in my twenties. I don't know how old you are, but if you have a ten-year-old, that's probably about when you got started, isn't it?"

"I'm thirty-four, so yeah. Ryder was born when I was twenty-four."

"And that means that you have the chance to be around to see your kids at forty, at fifty or sixty. To know your grandchildren and maybe even your great-grandchildren. That's how I want it, too. Family is the most important thing to me. As far as I'm concerned, that's what life is about."

"But isn't it about doing all that with a partner?" he asked, still sounding baffled.

"Ideally. But look at you—there are no guarantees that even if you start out with a partner you'll end up with one."

"Yeah…" he conceded a bit dourly. "It's just…single-parenthood is a tough road. I'm never sure whether or not I might be dropping the ball in some way. Especially lately…"

Nina was curious about that, but out of the blue a pain more severe than any she'd felt yet hit her, pulling her away from the back of the seat.

Dallas sat up just as quickly, angled toward her and put an arm around her from behind.

"It's okay," he said in that deep masculine voice that she was finding tremendously soothing. "Just ride it out. Don't fight it. Breathe…"

She tried to do all of that, but this pain was sharp. She closed her eyes against it and the renewed fear that came with it.

"It's okay," he repeated. "It'll all be okay."

Then she felt him press his lips to her temple in a sweet, tender, bolstering kiss that she knew had to have been a purely involuntary reaction of his own when he didn't know what else to say to her.

The pain disappeared as fast as it had come on, and Nina wilted.

The fact that she wilted against Dallas Traub was also not something she thought about before it just seemed to happen.

But he held her as if it were something he'd done a million times before, and it seemed perfectly natural for her head to rest against his chest.

"There was a long time between pains," Nina said when she was able. "I thought they'd stopped."

"It's good that they aren't coming with any kind of regularity. Real labor is like clockwork. Maybe these are just muscle spasms."

The baby had been moving and kicking normally as they were talking so it didn't seem as if it was in distress, but still, there was nothing heartening about the situation.

"But you know," Dallas said in a lighter vein. "If I end up delivering this guy you'll have to name him after me—Dallas Traub Crawford."

That did make Nina laugh. "Both of our families would freak out over *that*," she said. "And I haven't let them tell me if the baby is a boy or a girl—I want to be surprised."

"The name still works even if it's a girl."

"Dallas Crawford." Nina tried it on for size and then laughed again. "Let's see…first I had to convince everyone that Leo isn't the father, that I actually had artificial insemination. Then we'll throw you into the mix? I can just imagine the rumors."

"Rust Creek'd be talking about it for years."

"And both of our families would probably stop speaking to us for consorting with the enemy."

"Seems possible," Dallas agreed with a laugh of his own.

Headlights suddenly appeared through the snow, coming from the direction of town, and within moments a vehicle pulled up beside them.

"What did I tell you? Help has arrived," Dallas said.

Nina sat up and away from him, regretting the loss of his arm around her when he let go of her and turned to open the door.

Gage Christensen, the local sheriff, was standing just outside.

"You out here joyriding?" Dallas joked, but Nina heard the relief in his tone.

"When the storm hit your mother called the farm where you were delivering hay to find out if you'd left there. They said you had, and since you hadn't gotten home, she called me."

Dallas glanced over his shoulder at Nina. "What did I tell you? The thought of being stuck for too long with my three boys got the troops sent out to find me in a hurry."

Then, back to Gage Christensen, he said. "I have Nina Crawford in here and I think she needs to get to the hospital in Kalispell—the sooner the better…."

So he was clearly more worried about her condition than he'd originally let on.

"Looks to me like I can pull around behind you and push you forward enough to get you going. Then I'll do the hospital run," Gage Christensen said.

"Why don't you get me out of this ditch and just follow us? It's probably not a great idea to move Nina but I'd like to know we have some backup. And maybe after the storm someone can come out here and get her SUV."

Nina was surprised that Dallas hadn't jumped at the opportunity to be off the hook. But she appreciated that he hadn't, that he still seemed concerned for her.

"Let's see what we can do," the sheriff said, returning to his own vehicle.

Turning back to Nina, Dallas grasped her upper arm in one of those big hands and squeezed. "Just relax, we'll be on the way before you know it," he said, once more sounding confident.

Nina nodded, relieved that they were going to get out of there.

Then Dallas left, closed the rear door, and came in from the passenger side of the front seat to slide across and restart the engine, turning on the heat again.

It wasn't long before there was a slight bump to the rear of Dallas's truck. Then there was the sound of spinning tires and the feel of the truck inching forward until Dallas's wheels caught enough traction to move onto the road.

"Now we're cooking," he said victoriously.

"My purse—I should have my insurance card," Nina said as it became clear that they actually were going to be able to travel.

"I'll get it," he said, coming to a slow stop, then rushing out of the truck's cab into the storm again to return with her oversize hobo bag and her keys.

"Thank you," she said when he handed everything to her over the front seat. Then, a bit emotionally, she added, "Thank you for everything today...."

"Let's just get you to the hospital," he said, putting the truck into gear and setting off cautiously into the still-blinding blizzard.

Watching the back of his head as he drove, Nina couldn't help marveling at the fact that she was continuing to be looked after by none other than Dallas Traub.

Personable, kind, caring, strong, reassuring and more handsome than she'd ever realized before, he couldn't know how glad she was that he hadn't merely handed her off to the sheriff.

And in that moment she couldn't help wondering why it was that she was supposed to hate him.

Chapter 2

"Is anyone here for Nina Crawford?"

Dallas got to his feet the moment he heard that. He was in the waiting area for the emergency room of the hospital in Kalispell, where he'd been since arriving with Nina and having her whisked away.

"I'm Dr. Axel," the woman introduced herself.

Dallas wasn't sure whether or not to admit he wasn't family but before he could say anything the woman continued.

"Nina and the baby are doing fine. The pains she was having were the result of hitting the steering wheel, not labor. There's no indication that she's about to deliver. We've done an ultrasound and the baby looks good, plus Nina is hooked up to a fetal monitor and there are no signs of any kind of distress."

"Great!" Dallas said, relief ringing clear.

"As I'm sure you know," the doctor went on, "Nina is at thirty-five weeks so birth at this stage—while inadvisable—would still likely not pose unusual problems for mom or baby should something change suddenly. But with the storm and the difficulties on the roads, getting her back here in a hurry might pose a problem and I'd rather err on the side of safety. So we're keeping her overnight. That way we can continue to monitor things and watch them both, just in case."

"Sure."

"She's being taken to a room now—if you check with one of the people at the desk they'll be able to tell you the number."

Dallas thanked the doctor, then he went to the reception desk, gave Nina's name and learned what room she'd been taken to.

It was only after he had that information that he wondered if he *should* stay.

After all, he *wasn't* family.

But while Gage Christensen had promised to notify the Crawfords of the accident and tell them Nina's whereabouts, none of them had arrived yet. Despite the fact that the blizzard had stopped and only a light snow was falling, the roads still weren't great, so there was no surprise there. And Dallas didn't like the thought of Nina being alone, even if everything was okay.

So he opted to stay. Just the way he'd opted to stay after getting Nina here, despite the sheriff pointing out that he'd done enough, that there was nothing more he could do now that she was in the hands of the professionals, and that he might as well go home to his own family.

His family—his boys—were being well taken care of by his parents, all of whom he'd talked to while he was in the waiting room. Everything was going on as usual. But for now, without him, Nina had no one.

And he just couldn't bring himself to leave her.

So he went to the elevator, got in and hit the button for her floor.

The maternity floor.

He knew it well. He'd been there for the birth of each of his three sons. With Laurel...

That memory wrenched his gut. The way countless other memories had during the past year.

The past year of hell...

It just wasn't easy.

Not waking up to find his wife had left him.

Not raising three kids on his own.

Not dealing with his own anger and grief and sometimes rage and despair.

Not dealing with his sons' emotions, which were sometimes right on the surface and other times came out so subtly he missed them until it was too late.

Not going on, living in the same town where they'd both grown up, being where almost everything in their life had happened, revisiting places like this hospital, where events had come about that were apparently not as meaningful to his ex-wife as they were to him....

Yeah, *hell* pretty much described it. And he was just trying to work his way through the emotional muck, in much the same way that Rust Creek Falls was still working its way through the muck left from the flood.

But he had confidence that Rust Creek Falls would get through its reconstruction and come out on the other end. He still wasn't altogether sure about himself. Or about Ryder or Jake or Robbie.

When the elevator arrived on the maternity floor, he found Nina's room without a problem and breathed a sigh of relief. It was a private room on a different corridor than where new mothers were located.

If he'd had to walk into one of the same rooms Laurel had been in with any of the boys he didn't know if he could have done it. He could only push himself so far, even though he was doing his damnedest to get out of this hell he'd been in since Laurel had left.

Just pretend you're okay even if you aren't—that was what he'd decided he had to do. And maybe if he pretended he wasn't buried under the blues, he'd finally start to actually see daylight again.

But one way or another, he'd already made an early New Year's resolution—he was determined to spare his family and friends any more of what he'd been wallowing in for the past twelve months. No more telling everyone to beware of love, to avoid relationships. No more being the naysayer as he watched people couple up. He'd at least keep his mouth shut.

The door from the corridor was open and the curtain around the bed was only partially drawn so he could see that Nina was asleep, and he reconsidered staying once again. After the day they'd had she was probably exhausted and she could well sleep until her family got there, or even until morning.

But he really, really didn't want to go yet. Just in case.

So he went silently to the visitor's chair and sat down, settling in to study Nina rather than thinking more about the other times he'd been on the maternity floor or about the misery of this past year.

Nina Crawford...

Jeez, she was beautiful.

Her long, shiny hair was the color of chestnuts and it fanned out like silk on the pillow.

Her skin was pure porcelain.

Her nose was perfect, thin and sleek, and just slightly pointed at the end.

Her mouth was petal-pink, her lips just lush enough to make a man want to kiss them.

Her face was finely boned with a chin that was well-defined, cheekbones that were high and sculpted, and a brow that was straight and not too high, not too narrow.

And even though her eyes were closed and her long, thick lashes dusted her cheeks, he had a vivid recollection of just how big and brown they were—doelike and sparkling, they were the dark, rich color of coffee.

Yep, beautiful. Exquisitely, delicately beautiful.

Without the doctor telling him, he would have never guessed that she was as far along as she was. By now, with all three of the boys, Laurel had not looked the way Nina did. Not that he hadn't thought Laurel was beautiful, because he had.

He was a man of nature, and he'd genuinely thought the entire process had that feel to it—natural and as beautiful as a sunrise evolving out of the dark of night.

But the more weight his ex-wife had gained, the more unhappy she'd become. Even more unhappy than she'd been during the rest of the marriage she'd never really been happy in....

Laurel was the last thing he wanted to think about, though, so he sealed off the memory and focused on Nina, who honestly did make true the adage about pregnant women glowing.

Or maybe that was just the way she looked all the time....

Since he'd never noticed her before, he couldn't actually be the judge.

Although sitting there now, studying her, he wondered *why* he'd never noticed her before. How could anyone who looked the way she did have gone *un*noticed?

She was only twenty-five—that was probably a factor because she was too young for him to have paid attention to. Plus he'd been so involved with his marriage—first in the early throes of love, and then trying to save it—that he hadn't really paid attention to any other females. And even as an adult, Nina's being a Crawford just automatically clumped her together with the rest of her family, who had all been cast under the shadow of contempt. Put it all together and he supposed that he'd just been blind to her.

But he wasn't blind to her anymore.

At that moment he was sorry he wasn't sitting as close to her as he'd been in the backseat of his truck. With the blanket over the two of them. With his arm around her—the way it had been when he'd put it there without even thinking about it.

The same way he'd kissed her without even thinking about it....

A Crawford. He'd kissed a Crawford.

A pregnant Crawford.

This had been a very strange day....

But still, thinking about it, here he was wishing he was back there. Stuck in a blizzard. At risk of having to deliver that baby.

Because it had somehow been nice there like that. With her.

It had been the best time he'd had in a very, very long while....

Okay, maybe he'd lost it. The best time he'd had in a long time, and it had been in that situation, with a Crawford?

That was crazy.

And yet, true...

Because she was something, this Nina Crawford.

Even under the worst circumstances, out there stuck in the snow, there had still been something positive and affirming about her. Strong. He'd known she was worried and scared, and even in the face of that she hadn't bemoaned anything, she'd held her head high about making the choice she'd made to have that baby on her own, and she was just...

Something.

Something a whole lot better than he'd been for the past year since his divorce.

Something a whole lot better than the cranky naysayer he sometimes felt as though he'd turned into.

She was a positive force. He was a negative one.

Figured. The Crawfords and the Traubs—

oil and water. That was how they'd always been. How they always would be. Except that he and Nina hadn't been oil and water today.

Not that that meant anything. Or mattered.

Even if she wasn't a Crawford, he thought, she was still only twenty-five and pregnant, while he was thirty-four and had three kids. Nothing about any of that put them on the same page. And people who weren't on the same page couldn't—or at least shouldn't—come together. He'd learned that the hard way with Laurel.

Not that what had gone on today was anything like he and Nina Crawford *coming together,* he told himself when his own thoughts alarmed him a little.

He just felt responsible for her for the moment. Because he was the other party involved in the near-collision that had put her in the hospital.

There wasn't any more to it than that.

If he could just stop recalling every minute of being alone with her in his backseat.

"Dallas Traub? What are you doing here?"

Now *that* was a Crawford that Dallas recognized.

"Nate," Dallas answered in a whisper, glancing up to find Nina's brother Nathan

Crawford in the doorway with their parents—Todd and Laura, who had also been front and center through the recent mayoral election in support of their son—who had lost the race to Dallas's brother, Collin.

Dallas stood instantly to face them. "Didn't Gage tell you what happened?" he whispered, both in response and as a signal to keep voices low.

"He said Nina went off the road and had to be brought here. He didn't say anything about you," the matriarch of the Crawford family whispered back harshly, obviously having taken the cue.

But the attempt to keep things quiet was already too late because from the bed Nina said, "Stop. Dallas isn't to blame. It was all my fault. I couldn't see him coming until it was too late and I'd pulled out in front of him. We both swerved to keep from crashing."

"Still bad enough. What are you doing here now?" Todd Crawford demanded.

"Daddy, Dallas has been great!" Nina informed her father. "He took care of me until the sheriff got there and even then he didn't let Gage move me, and he had Gage follow us to make sure we got here all right. And here he is, even now!"

Dr. Axel joined the group then and Nina seemed to seize the sudden presence of the obstetrician as help in mediating, because she said, "Hi, Dr. Axel. Could you maybe take my family out in the hallway and let them know what's going on with the baby?"

The doctor did as requested, herding the other Crawfords from the room.

"Thought I needed to be rescued, did you?" Dallas said with a laugh, moving to stand directly at the foot of the bed.

"Three against one—bad odds," she answered, sounding groggy and worn-out.

"I didn't want to leave you by yourself," Dallas explained his continuing presence.

"That was thoughtful." She gestured in the direction her family had gone. "I'm sorry that was your reward for being so nice."

"No big deal," he assured her, finding that what *was* feeling like a big deal to him was the idea that he was going to have to leave her now....

"Everything with you and the baby is fine, you know that, right?" he said then.

"I do. I'm giving you credit for that."

"Nah. I didn't do anything."

"You did—"

"I'm just glad you and the baby are okay."

"And that you didn't have to deliver it," Nina said with a smile that let him know she was teasing him.

"That, too," he agreed, laughing in return and basking in the warmth of that smile that he liked more than seemed possible.

"Is it still snowing?" she asked then.

"It is, but the wind stopped so it isn't as bad out there."

"You should get home, then. To your boys."

Dallas nodded. He did need to get home. He just couldn't figure out why he was so reluctant to leave Nina. Nina *Crawford,* he reminded himself, as if that would help. "I suppose your family can take over from here."

"They will. And everything is okay anyway, so there isn't really anything to take over. I'll lie in this bed and get waited on tonight, then go home tomorrow."

Again Dallas nodded, lingering. "I'm sorry for all of this. That it happened," he said, although that wasn't strictly the case. He *was* sorry for what had happened. Just not for the time he'd had with her *after* it had happened.

"I'm sorry, too," Nina said. "I'm sure you had better plans today than to end up stuck on the side of a road in a blizzard thinking you might have to turn your backseat into a delivery room, and then sitting at this hospital for the past four hours."

"Believe it or not, I've had worse days," he declared with a laugh.

The reappearance of her family and the doctor at the door made it clear that he had to go whether he liked it or not. "Anyway, since you're in good hands, I'll head for home."

"Thank you," Nina said in a tone that had some intimacy to it.

"Anytime," he answered with humor.

"Be careful going back."

"I will be," he promised.

And that was that.

But for another moment Dallas stayed there, still finding it oddly difficult to leave. To walk out and put this day behind him. To sever the connection that somehow seemed to have formed between them through the adversity they'd shared. To return to the way things had been before—to barely being aware that Nina Crawford existed.

He had to go, though. What else was he going to do? Especially when her family and doctor all came to stand around her bed, the Crawfords' scorn for him thick in the air as they pretended he was invisible.

He stole one last glance at Nina, whose big

brown eyes met his, who gave him a smile that spoke of the connection they'd made, if only for a little while today. Then he raised a palm to her in a goodbye wave and finally did manage to leave.

Wishing—for no reason he understood—that a lot of things might be different.

And realizing only as he got back on the elevator to go down to the lobby that for just a little while with her he hadn't felt so bad....

By Friday, Nina was home in her small apartment above the General Store and feeling good again. Better than ever, in fact. But she was still following doctor's orders not to return to work until Saturday.

Her mother had been hovering. Laura Crawford had even spent Thursday night with Nina. But over lunch Friday afternoon, when Laura was still there and giving no indication of leaving, Nina had convinced her that everything was back to normal, and that Laura should go home.

Once she had and Nina was alone, her thoughts turned to Dallas Traub.

Since Wednesday's near-collision she'd been finding it nearly impossible *not* to think about him and had used the presence of family to distract herself. But, finally left to her own devices, she couldn't seem to think about anything but the swaggeringly sexy, blue-eyed Traub with the great head of hair who had taken such kind and tender care of her.

She wanted to thank him again for everything he'd done on Wednesday.

That was all there was to her constant thoughts of him, she told herself. And it was reasonable to want to express her gratitude.

After all, not only had he put aside whatever petty differences their families had, but he'd gone out of his way for her at every juncture.

Until her family had arrived and been rude to him.

And even then he'd been calm and courteous. He'd absorbed their scorn and contempt with aplomb and without dishing out any of his own before he'd gone on his way.

She owed him more than gratitude, she decided.

But thanking him again was a start, in order to let him know just how much she appreciated everything.

And if she also felt the need to hear his voice again and make some kind—*any* kind—of contact with him?

Maybe it was an odd phenomenon where a person developed a sense of kinship with their rescuer.

That seemed possible.

It seemed more possible than any kind of alternative. Like wanting contact with him because she was attracted to him....

How crazy would that *be?* she asked herself.

Attracted to someone when she was eight months pregnant?

Attracted to a Traub?

Completely crazy, that's how crazy it would be.

And even more crazy still when she factored in his age.

That was the frosting on the cake.

Dallas was nine years older than she was, so even if she wasn't pregnant, and even if he wasn't a Traub, his age alone was enough for her to steer completely clear of him.

Leo had been ten years older than she was, and Nina had had enough of the disadvantages that came with a relationship with a wide gap in ages. Enough of accommodating and adapting and making all the adjustments because that age seemed to bring with it the privilege of some kind of seniority.

And Leo hadn't had kids.

Dallas Traub did. *Three* of them.

Kids only increased the need for any woman who got involved with him to be accommodating.

Involved?

She didn't know why Dallas Traub and involvement had even come in the same thought. Of course she wasn't and would never get *involved* with him!

She just wanted to talk to him, for crying out loud. And then maybe find a way to show her appreciation. Like with a fruit basket or something.

To reiterate her thanks. To apologize for the way her family had treated him.

It was all just the right thing, given what he'd done for her. Nothing more to it. Dallas had done her a huge kindness and service, and she owed him her gratitude.

And, hey, maybe if the two of them could treat each other courteously it could be the beginning of some kind of bridge between the two families, so that her child and his sons might not have to hate each other for no reason anyone could actually explain.

That was probably a stretch. The bad blood between the Traubs and the Crawfords had been going on for generations, and the mere act of reiterating her thanks to him wasn't likely to cure that.

But still, she felt compelled to make the phone call.

It required a few other calls to friends to get Dallas's cell phone number, but she finally did. When she dialed it he answered right away.

The sound of that deep, deep voice filled her with something she couldn't explain. Something warm and satisfying.

But she ignored the response and said, "Dallas? This is Nina Crawford."

He laughed. "You're the only Nina I know. Hi!" he added, sounding happy to hear from her. Which was somewhat of a relief because it *had* crossed her mind that, now that they weren't in dire straits, things between them might return to the normal state of affairs. At least, normal for *their* families.

"I've been thinking and thinking about you—how are you?" he asked immediately and in a tone that held only friendliness.

"I'm really good," she said. "I got home yesterday and can't work until tomorrow. But I feel fine and I would be downstairs doing everything I usually do right now if not for doctor's orders."

"Downstairs? In your store?"

"That's where I work," she answered with a laugh.

"I'm there now."

He was just downstairs?

Knowing he was that nearby sent a sense of elation through her. Strange as it seemed...

"I live in the apartment above the store," she informed him. "Want to come and see for yourself that—thanks to you—I'm faring very well?"

Nina had no idea where that had come from. It was nothing but impulse.

But Dallas didn't hesitate before he said, "I'd like that! How do I get there?"

"Go to the back of the store. There's a staircase behind Women's Sleepwear and Intimates—"

"The boys will love that," he said facetiously. Then he added, "Oh, I didn't think about that. My boys are with me. Maybe we shouldn't come up—"

"I'm kid-friendly," she assured. Then she laughed again. "I'd better be."

"You're sure you don't mind? And that you're well enough?"

"I'm sure. Come on up."

That was all the convincing it took for him to say eagerly, "Be right there."

Hanging up, Nina knew that it was absurd to be as excited as she was by the fact that she was about to get to see Dallas again right now.

But that's the way it was.

She was excited enough to make a quick detour to the nearest mirror to make sure her hair didn't need brushing and to hurriedly apply a little mascara and blush.

She was wearing jeans and a red turtleneck sweater that was long enough and just loose enough to accommodate her not-too-large belly. And while she was shoeless, her socks were red-and-green argyle for the holiday so she stayed in her stocking feet to open the door.

Dallas was there when she did, his fisted hand ready to knock.

"Whoa," he said, stopping short so she didn't get the knock in the face.

Nina couldn't help grinning at that first glimpse of him. Tall, broad-shouldered, wearing boots, jeans and that same suede coat over a plaid flannel shirt with the collar button open to expose a white T-shirt underneath it.

Rugged, masculine, rock-solid and drop-dead gorgeous—so her mind hadn't built him up to be more than he actually was, she thought. She'd been wondering if that might be the case.

"Come in! Take off your coats," she invited, stepping aside.

Dallas crossed the threshold, trailed by three boys of varying heights, all of them younger versions of him, with the same blue eyes hazed with gray, the same heads of thick brown hair, the same bone structure.

"This is Ryder." He began the introductions with a hand on the head of the tallest as they all removed their coats. "And Jake." Clearly the middle child. "And Robbie—"

"I just got to be six and I go to kinnergarten," Robbie announced.

"Then I'll bet your teacher is Willa Christensen," Nina said.

"No. It's my aunt Willa but in school I need to call her Mrs. Traub. Like me, Robbie Traub. But she's not my mom, she's my aunt since she married my Uncle Collin."

"Ah, that's right. I guess I sort of forgot that Willa married your brother," Nina said to Dallas.

"Lookit all this Christmas stuff! Lookit that tree!" Robbie said then, wasting no time moving into Nina's apartment to survey her many Christmas decorations.

"It is pretty festive in here," Dallas agreed.

"I love Christmas," Nina said before focusing on the other two boys, who were staying near to their father. "So Robbie is six. You're eight, Jake? And Ryder, you're ten, right?"

"Yeah," Jake confirmed while Ryder said nothing at all.

"Well, come on in. You can have a look around, too, if you want. There's a dish of candy canes and taffy—if it's all right with your dad you can help yourselves. And how would you all like some hot chocolate and Christmas cookies?"

"I would!" Robbie answered first.

"Me, too," Jake seconded.

Ryder merely shrugged his concession just before Dallas said, "What do you say?"

"I would, please," Robbie amended.

"Me, too, *please*." Jake added some attitude while a simple "Please" was muttered by Ryder as the older boys joined the younger in looking around and ultimately being drawn to the train that circled the tree skirt.

"Does this work?" Jake asked.

"It does. The switch is on the side of the

station house," Nina answered, closing the door behind them all.

"Watch what you're doing," Dallas warned his sons.

"It's okay," Nina told him. "They can't hurt anything. Like I said, kid-friendly."

She led the way into the kitchen portion of the big open room that included a fair-sized kitchen and dining area separated from the large living room by an island counter.

"This is a nice place. I didn't even know it was up here," Dallas said as Nina set about heating milk and adding cocoa and broken chocolate bars.

"It's where the first Crawfords in Rust Creek Falls lived when they started the store. A lot of us have taken advantage of it over the years. You can't beat the commute to work," she joked.

"You'll bring your baby home here?"

"I will. There are two bedrooms—the nursery is almost ready, I just have a few finishing touches to put on it. And living up here after the baby is born—even before I've actually gone back to work—will let me still oversee some things. Then when I *can* get back to business as usual, I'll have a nanny or a sitter here with the baby, but I'll be able to carry a baby monitor with me to listen in and I'll also be able to come up as many times a day as I want or need to."

"Handy," he agreed.

"I think it will be."

"And is this still going to be a house of sugar when you have your own kid?" he asked as she set iced cookies out on a plate and then brought the pan of hot chocolate from the stove.

He was teasing her again and it struck her that there was already some familiarity in it. Familiarity she liked...

"It's Christmas," she defended. "And the middle of the afternoon—I'm sure they had lunch and dinner is far enough away that this won't spoil their appetites."

"And they'll be so wired they won't have to ride home in the truck, they'll be able to run behind it," he joked before advising, "Give them all half cups of hot chocolate."

"Killjoy," Nina accused playfully. And slightly flirtatiously, though she didn't know where that had come from....

"Oh, so you've heard about how glum I've been the past year," he joked back, smiling that crooked smile that lifted one side of his agile-looking mouth higher than the other.

His eyes were intent on her, and the humor allowed them to share a moment that told Nina she wasn't alone in whatever it was she'd been feeling about him as her rescuer. That, regardless of the old feud between their families, things between the two of them were different now even if they were no longer in dire straits.

It pleased her. A lot.

Dallas took two mugs of hot chocolate in each of his big, capable hands, leaving Nina to carry the fifth and the plate of cookies into the living room. They set everything on her oval oak coffee table and the boys gathered around it, sitting on the floor while Nina and Dallas sat on her overstuffed black-and-gray buffalo-checked sofa.

After the boys tasted their hot chocolate and each took a cookie, Robbie looked to his father and said, "When are we gonna put up our tree?"

"You don't have a tree yet?" Nina asked, surprised.

"Dad's been too busy," Jake answered, disappointment and complaint ringing in his tone as the three boys carried their cookies and hot chocolate with them and went back to playing with the train.

"Busy and not much in the mood," Dallas confessed, quietly enough for the boys not to be able to hear.

"Scrooge," she teased him the same way.

"I'm not usually," he admitted, his voice still low and echoing with sorrow. "But this year... I don't know. It's felt all year like this family has been left sort of in shreds and I'm not quite sure how to sew it back together again. Or if I'm even up to it."

"Kids need their holidays kept, no matter what," Nina insisted.

But she couldn't be too hard on him, considering that this was the anniversary of the end of his marriage and it couldn't be an easy time for him.

So rather than criticizing any more, she decided to fall back on the reason she'd contacted him in the first place.

"I called because I wanted to thank you again for helping me on Wednesday," she said, setting her own cup of hot chocolate on the coffee table and breaking off a section of a bell-shaped cookie. "I also wanted to apologize for the way my family treated you at the hospital."

"I'm sure they were worried and upset about you and the baby—"

Robbie overheard that and perked up to look at them over his shoulder. "You're gonna have a baby? I thought you just liked beer."

Confused, Nina looked from the youngest Traub to Dallas and found Dallas grimacing. "We met an old friend of mine earlier today. He was a lot heavier than the last time I saw him and I razzed him about his beer belly."

"Ah…" Nina said.

"But you," Dallas went on in a hurry, obviously doing damage control. "It doesn't seem like you've gained an ounce anywhere but baby—you really look…well, beautiful…"

It sounded as if he genuinely meant that— not like the gratuitous things that often came with people talking about her pregnancy. And that, too, pleased Nina. And when their eyes met once again, when she really could see that he didn't find anything about her condition off-putting at all, and when Nina had the feeling that there was suddenly no one else in the world but the two of them, it made her all warm inside.

But there were other people in the world, in the room, in fact. His kids.

And just then Ryder said, "I need to get to Tyler's."

Dallas seemed to draw up short, as if he,

too, had been lost in that moment between them and was jolted out of it by his eldest son's reminder.

"His friend Tyler is having a sleepover," Dallas explained. "And I still need to pick up a few things downstairs—our houses and the main barns were spared by the flood but some of the outbuildings and lean-tos had some damage. I thought we'd fixed every-thing but the blizzard showed us more weak spots, and I came for some lumber and some nails." He paused, smiled slyly, then said, "And I figured if I came here rather than going to Kalispell I'd get the chance to ask how you're doing…"

"I'm doing fabulously," she answered as if he'd asked her.

The sly smile widened to a grin that lit up his handsome face.

"I told Tyler I'd be at his house by now," Ryder persisted.

Dallas rolled his eyes but allowed his atten-tion to be dragged away. "Okay, cups to the kitchen," he ordered in a tone that sounded reluctant.

"I'll take care of it," Nina said.

"Not a chance." Dallas overruled her, even cleaning up after her by taking her hot chocolate mug, too, and leaving her to merely follow behind them all with the cookie plate.

Once the cups were rinsed and in the sink, and coats were replaced, Nina went with them to the apartment door, opening it for them.

The boys immediately went out and headed for the stairs.

"Wait for me right there," Dallas warned as he lingered with Nina.

Then he glanced at her again with the same look in his blue eyes that had been there when he'd told her she was beautiful. "I'm really glad to see that you're okay. Better than okay."

"It's all thanks to you," she told him.

He flashed that one-sided smile again. "All me, huh? Doctors, the hospital—none of that had anything to do with it?"

"They just did the checkup. It was you who got me through the worst. And then took heat from my family for it."

"Just happy to help," he said as if he meant that, too.

"I owe you…."

"Nah. You don't owe me anything."

Nina merely smiled. "I'm glad you came up today."

"Me, too."

"Dad!" Ryder chastised from the top of the stairs.

"In a minute," Dallas said without taking his eyes off Nina. He was clearly reluctant to leave. "Guess I better go. Take care of yourself. And that baby," he advised.

"I will," she agreed.

Then he had no choice but to go, and Nina leaned out of her apartment door so she could watch him join his sons, so she could watch the four of them descend the steps.

And all the while she was still smiling to herself.

Because she'd thought of a much, much better thank-you gift than a fruit basket.

A gift that would put her in the company of Dallas Traub one more time.

Chapter 3

"You have to be kidding. You want me to tie a Christmas tree to the top of your SUV so you can surprise some *Traubs* with it?"

It was after five on Sunday. Nate had dropped by the store just before closing and Nina had asked her brother to do her a favor so the teenager who was running the Christmas tree lot didn't have to stay late to do it.

"Dallas needs a tree," she told Nate matter-of-factly. "And it's the least I can do after Wednesday. It's a thank-you Christmas tree."

"Thanks for running you off the road and nearly killing you?"

"*I* pulled out in front of *him*," Nina repeated

what she'd said to her family numerous times since the near-collision. "I don't know what I would have done without him."

"You wouldn't have ended up in a ditch."

"Nathan!" Nina said in a louder voice, attempting to get through to her brother. "Dallas Traub saved me and my baby!"

Okay, maybe that was somewhat of an exaggeration, but in the thick of things on Wednesday, Dallas *had* felt like a lifesaver.

"I want to repay him with this Christmas tree," she insisted.

"We don't owe any Traub anything," Nate said, scowling at her.

"I owe Dallas," Nina said firmly and succinctly.

She'd always been a strong, independent person who acted on her own instincts and answered whatever beliefs, desires or drives she might have, even if they went against popular opinion. Like having this baby on her own. And like giving Dallas and his boys a Christmas tree whether anyone in her stubborn family approved or not.

"If you're bound and determined to give a Traub a tree then have it delivered," her brother reasoned. "Why do you have to take it out to him yourself?"

"I *want* to take it out to him myself," she said defensively, trying not to think about just how much she wanted to do this herself. "He inconvenienced *him*self and even put himself in danger by taking me into Kalispell during a blizzard when he could have just let the sheriff do it and gone home to his own family. Delivering my gift in person is only right."

Which she believed.

But she also couldn't stop thinking about Dallas and wanting to see him again—that was a strong part of her determination to do the delivery herself, too.

Of course, she told herself that now that she'd met Dallas's kids, now that she knew Dallas was having trouble getting into the holiday spirit those kids deserved—the holiday spirit that every kid deserved—it just seemed appropriate that she step up and provide it. In her time of need, Dallas had come to the rescue. Now, in this small way, maybe she could come to his.

And getting to spend a little time with him in the process was inconsequential and meaningless—that was what she kept telling herself.

"Some Traub will probably shoot you on sight when you drive onto their property," Nate said.

Nina rolled her eyes. "This isn't the Wild West anymore. Besides, I've been asking around at the store yesterday and today to get an idea of the actual arrangement of the houses at the Triple T ranch. Dallas and his boys have their own place that sits on one of the borders of the ranch. I can get to it from a side road without going any farther onto the property."

"He's still likely to shoot you," Nathan muttered. Her brother's grumblings about angry Traubs were so ridiculous they made Nina laugh. Regardless of the conflicts between the Crawford family and the Traub family, her own current feelings about Dallas—and his sons—didn't hold any animosity. And she was reasonably certain that Dallas didn't bear her ill will at this point, either.

Certain enough that she had no compunctions about showing up at his doorstep unannounced to surprise him with the tree. And some ornaments and some lights and just a bit of Christmas cheer that her brother didn't know she already had loaded into the rear of her SUV.

"Yes, I'm sure Dallas went to all the trouble of saving me only to turn around and shoot me today," she said facetiously in answer to her brother's comment.

"I don't like it, Nina," Nate said then, seriously, solemnly, showing genuine concern. "You know how things are with the Traubs—they're the enemy."

"In what?" Nina challenged. "Some stupid generations-old family feud? They're the Hatfields and we're the McCoys? Or vice versa? I'm beginning to think that that's just plain dumb."

"You might not think it was so *dumb* if it was you who just lost that race for mayor to a *Traub*."

Nathan couldn't seem to say the name without rancor—actually no one in her family ever could—but still Nina thought maybe she was being insensitive to her brother. Nate had poured his heart and soul into the campaign for the office of Rust Creek's mayor and then lost. To Collin Traub.

"I understand, and I don't blame you for having hard feelings about losing the run for mayor," she assured Nathan. "But this is something just between Dallas and me. Separate from any family squabbles or defeats or any of the rest of it. After all, he did *me* a great kindness separate from everything. Or would you have rather *he* had looked at the situation on Wednesday and left me to fend for myself because I'm a Crawford?"

"No…" Nate admitted with clear reluctance. "I just don't think you owe him anything for it."

"If it had been someone else who did what he did, would you feel the same way?" Nina reasoned.

Her brother scowled again but refused to answer.

Nina knew why and said, "No, you wouldn't feel the same way. You and Mom and Dad would have rushed into the hospital room and fallen all over yourselves thanking him. And right now you'd have that tree tied to my luggage rack and you'd probably be telling me to tell whoever how grateful you all are that he helped me out."

Nate didn't respond to that but he did hoist the tall pine tree up onto her luggage rack and reach down for the bungee cords to hold it there.

After securing the cords and yanking on the tree to make sure it was held tight, Nate got down off her running board and returned to her, still frowning his disapproval.

"It's a good thing we've had nothing but sunshine since Wednesday and the roads are clear or I wouldn't let you do this," he said.

As if he could stop her.

Nina refrained from saying that and instead said, "But the roads are clear, there isn't another storm in sight and thanks for that." She nodded toward the tree now fastened to the roof of her SUV.

Nate would only accept her gratitude with a shrug, letting her know he still didn't approve of what she was doing or of her having contact with any Traub.

But Nina merely kissed her brother on the cheek and sent him on his way.

So that she could be on her way, too.

Even as she tried to contain the wave of excitement that flooded through her at the thought that she was on her way to seeing Dallas again....

Dallas's house was a large two-story that sat not too far back from the side road that bordered the Traub's Triple T ranch.

Nina was glad to see the glow of lights behind the curtained windows when she pulled up in front of it. On the drive from Rust Creek Falls proper it had occurred to her that he might be having Sunday dinner with his parents, who lived in the main house on the property. But if the lights were on, he was probably there. Which meant she was going to get to see him again after all, and that made her happier than she wanted to admit.

Turning off her engine, she got out of her SUV and went up the four steps onto the porch, crossing it to get to the front door.

There were butterflies in her stomach suddenly, as the thought flitted through her mind that Dallas might not be happy to see her. What if she'd merely been enjoying a temporary truce?

Or what if his parents or his brothers were *here* for Sunday dinner?

Even if things were still okay between her and Dallas, Nina had no doubt that his family's response to her would be as bad as her family's response to him had been. And the thought of that put a damper on what she had planned.

But she'd come to do this and she couldn't let these last-minute concerns stop her. She had to at least find out what was going on inside that house. She couldn't just turn tail and run because things might be different than what she'd envisioned. So she raised a finger to the doorbell and rang it.

Holding her breath.

Then the door opened, and Dallas was standing there—somehow looking even taller, more broad-shouldered and even more hand-some, too, despite the fact that he was obviously in stay-at-home clothes that included faded, ages-old jeans and a gray sweatshirt with the sleeves pushed to midforearms.

He also had a kitchen towel slung over one of those broad shoulders and a shadow of beard on the lower half of his face that gave him an extra-rugged appeal Nina tried not to notice. Instead, she focused on the fact that his expression showed shock, then pleased shock as his eyebrows arched and he gave her a glimpse of that lopsided smile of his.

"Nina!"

"Hi. I hope this isn't a bad time."

His eyebrows arched higher, as if to ask, "A bad time for what?"

She nodded over her shoulder at her car. "I was going to get you a fruit basket or something to say thanks, but after Friday I thought a Christmas tree, some decorations and a few other holiday things were a better idea. And if you're up for it, I'd like to help you trim the tree and get some cheer going for your boys."

The arched eyebrows dipped into an almost-frown. "I can't let you do all that," he said.

"You can't let me say thank you?"

"You've said thank you. A couple of times."

He seemed kind of down tonight and that only made Nina more determined to do this.

"Still, what you did was huge to me, and I want to do this for you to show you how much I appreciated it. For you and the boys…" She added the boys at the end because for some reason there seemed to be an undertone of intimacy in her voice that she wanted to dispel.

"Are you even supposed to be out? Let alone carting Christmas trees around and decorating them for people?" Dallas asked then.

"I was back at work yesterday and today without any limitations, and I feel great. I don't know if it's supposed to be this way this close to the end, but I have a ton of energy—some to spare—and I'd really like to do this."

"Decorate a tree for me?"

"For you and the boys," she said, qualifying this time because there was a hint of intimacy in *his* voice now, and regardless of how excited she was to be looking up into his oh-so-handsome face she was also warning herself to keep things in perspective.

After a brief moment of seeming to consider what she was offering, Dallas shrugged in a way that made her think he was shrugging off some of his low spirits. Then he laughed a little and said, "Well, okay, I guess. If you're up for it."

"I am. If you'll get the tree off the car, I'll get the stuff out of the back—I brought a tree stand so you can just plunk it into that and we can get going."

"Yes, ma'am," he said with a wider smile at the take-charge attitude she was showing, the take-charge attitude that wasn't too different than what he'd shown on Wednesday in the blizzard.

Then he called over his shoulders for his sons to come and put on their coats while he removed the dish towel from his shoulder, slung it over the banister on the staircase behind him and thrust his arms into the largest of the four coats hanging on hooks beside the door.

"Lead the way…" he suggested to Nina as the boys came to the door like a tiny herd of elephants, their curiosity piqued, as well.

"Coats!" Dallas ordered a second time, explaining what was happening as the boys put them on and they all joined Nina on the porch.

"You brought us a Christmas tree?" Robbie exclaimed as they went out to the SUV.

"I did," Nina confirmed. "And a few other things that you can help me carry in while your dad and your brothers get the tree down."

"I been wantin' a tree!" Robbie said as if it were a revelation.

"Now you'll have one," Nina said with a laugh.

Even the oldest boy—Ryder, who had been so solemn on Friday when they'd met—seemed to perk up at the prospect of decorating for Christmas. And the more childish side of middle-son, Jake—who Nina had already realized liked to play it tough—was revealed as the two older boys aided their father in getting the tree unlashed from the roof of the SUV.

"Go on in and get out of the cold," Dallas commanded Nina when she and Robbie had taken the sacks from her rear cargo compartment. "The family room is to the left—that's where we put the tree."

Thinking more of the little boy than of herself, Nina did as she'd been told.

Inside the house, Nina took off her coat and so did Robbie—dropping his on the floor in his excitement to take the sacks into the other room and see what was in them.

Still in the entry, Nina picked up the child's coat and replaced it on the hook it had come from. Then she draped her own jacket over the newel post at the foot of the wide staircase that led to the second level of the house rather than taking someone else's hook.

She was wearing a turtleneck fisherman's-knit cable sweater that reached to midthigh of the skinny jeans she had on with her fur-lined, calf-high boots. After making sure the sweater wasn't bunched up over her rear end, she took the dish towel from where Dallas had set it over the banister and went in the direction Robbie had gone—to the left of the staircase.

The family room was a wide-open space paneled in a rustic wood, with man-sized leather furniture arranged around the entertainment center and the stone fireplace beside it.

Nina took the dish towel into the kitchen that was in the rear portion of the same area, separated from it only by a big round table surrounded by eight ladder-backed chairs.

On the counter beside the sink were four TV dinners with most of their contents left uneaten, and Nina wondered how often Dallas served frozen meals like that, hoping it wasn't too often. And hoping, too, that the whole household hadn't been feeling so sad tonight that none of them had felt like eating.

She left the dish towel folded neatly on the other side of the double sink and went to Robbie to help unload the bags she'd brought, explaining as she took things out what they were intended for.

"Dad! We have lights and tinsel and ornaments and these sparkly balls and candy canes, and Nina's gonna make us apple cider to drink while we put the tree up!" Robbie announced when his father and brothers carried the evergreen into the family room.

"I can see that," Dallas answered as he leaned the tree against a wall.

When the other boys were following Dallas's instructions to take his coat and theirs to hang up, and Robbie was still engrossed in emptying the bags, Nina said in an aside to Dallas, "I brought a bunch of new ornaments in case you didn't want memories raised with ones you used before...."

"Good idea. We can decide later what we might want to add and what we might not."

The older boys returned then. At Nina's suggestion Christmas music was turned on as she heated the cider and put it into mugs, and everyone got busy putting up the tree and decorating Dallas's house.

Nina half expected Dallas to merely sit on the sofa and watch her and the boys do the decorating, because in the four years she'd been with Leo, that was what he'd done. Christmas spirit seemed to have been something he'd out-grown, and while he'd assured her that he en-joyed the sight of a well-lit tree, he'd refused to exert the energy to actually decorate it.

But Dallas pitched in and did every bit as much as she did until the room was deco-rated—not quite as elaborately as Nina's apartment, but enough so that it looked very festive.

When all the work was done, Robbie de-manded that all the lights be turned off ex-cept for the tree lights, and that they all stand back to see how the tree looked in the dark. It looked beautiful, and Nina had the sense that the activity and the addition of the holiday cheer had lifted some of the cloud from the household. If not permanently, then at least for the time being.

Then Dallas said, "Tomorrow is a school day and you guys are late getting to sleep. Tell Nina thank-you for all of this and then upstairs to showers and pajamas and bed."

Ryder and Jake thanked her perfuncto-rily, but Robbie gave her an impromptu hug around the middle to accompany his expres-sion of gratitude. Then the boys went up the stairs in a thunderous retreat that seemed louder than a mere three kids could cause, and Nina and Dallas were suddenly alone.

"This was a really, really nice thing you did," Dallas said when the noise had dwindled to thumps and bumps overhead. He seemed inordinately grateful. As grateful as she'd been for his help during the blizzard. As grateful as if she'd done something for him that he just hadn't had it in him to do on his own.

"I wanted to do it," Nina assured him.

"Now sit and catch your breath," he insisted. "I'll reheat the cider and have another cup with you."

Better judgment told Nina to decline, to just head for home. She'd done what she'd come to do and she should just leave.

But she couldn't deny herself a few minutes alone with Dallas now that the work was finished and the boys were elsewhere.

So she sat on the big overstuffed leather sofa across from the Christmas tree that they'd set beside the fireplace.

She enjoyed the view of her handiwork and how much more cheerful the room looked while Dallas microwaved refills of cider for just the two of them. Then he brought the mugs and joined her.

Nina was at one end of the long couch, and after handing her the mug he sat on the opposite end. Far, far away.

Or, at least, that was how it seemed.

But it was good, Nina told herself. Because even if she was liking that scruff of beard on his face a little too much and thinking that it was sooo sexy, sitting at a distance from each other proved that there was nothing more to this than two relatively new acquaintances sharing a friendly evening together topped off by a cup of cider.

She took a sip of hers and said, "I wasn't exactly sure what I'd find when I came out here. You know, a Crawford setting foot on the Traub's Triple T ranch…"

"You thought you might be shot on sight?" Dallas joked, gazing at her over his own mug just before he took a drink, too.

"That's what Nate thought—he loaded the tree onto the car for me. I gave him grief for saying such a dumb thing, but I have to admit that I was glad when I found someone at the store today who could tell me which place out here was yours so I didn't have to go to the main house and ask. I sort of figured if I did I'd run into the same kind of wrath from your family that you got from mine."

"At least the hospital was a public place—that probably made it a little safer."

"But obviously not much," Nina said.

"I can't imagine Nathan was any too happy to load up a Christmas tree for you to bring to me," Dallas said then.

Nina shrugged her concession to that. "Losing the election to your brother *has* riled up my family all over again. I'm sure you know how that goes."

"Oh, I know. The slightest thing that happens with a Crawford and everyone on my side is up in arms."

"But it's gotten me to thinking…" Nina mused. "And it occurred to me that I don't even know for sure what started the Crawfords and the Traubs hating each other in the first place. Do you know?" she asked, having wondered a great deal about that since Wednesday when she'd discovered that she couldn't find a single thing wrong with Dallas. When, in fact, she could only find things more right than she wanted them to be.

"I've been thinking a lot about that, too," Dallas admitted. "Here you are, a nice person, great to be around—" and if the warmth in his gaze meant anything, he didn't hate the way she looked, either "—and I keep wondering why I'm supposed to think you're the devil incarnate just because you're a Crawford. But to tell you the truth, I don't know, either."

"I know there's been a history of Crawfords and Traubs competing for the same public positions—like this last election for mayor," Nina said.

"Right. There have been Traubs and Crawfords vying for the sheriff's job and city council seats along the way—I remember our fathers both running for an empty seat on the city council when I was a teenager."

"And that time my dad won—I'd forgotten that he sat on the city council for a while back then," Nina said.

"But there's always a winner and a loser in those things—sometimes in favor of a Traub, sometimes in favor of a Crawford—"

"And then there are hard feelings on the part of whichever side loses," Nina finished for him.

"Sure," Dallas agreed. "Plus I think I remember hearing something about a romance—a long, *long* time ago, when Rust Creek was nothing but cowboys and farmers. I think there was a story about a Traub and a Crawford both wanting the same woman, or something. And when neither of them got her they blamed each other...."

"I hadn't even heard that one," Nina said, laughing again. "I did hear one once about a business deal gone wrong, but all I know for sure is that whenever I've asked *why* the Crawfords and the Traubs hate each other it's started a tirade against the Traubs without any real answer. But it sounds like it's a matter of the Traubs and the Crawfords being *too* much alike and wanting the same things over and over again."

"It does, doesn't it?" Dallas agreed, laughing with her. "But at this point it just seems silly to me."

Nina was so glad to hear him say that. Probably because it was how she felt, as well, she told herself. It probably didn't have anything to do with the fact that she was enjoying being there with him so much, or the fact that she kept remembering how he'd taken care of her during the blizzard and the feel of him carrying her to his truck, the comforting feel of his arm around her when she'd had pain.

The feel of that kiss he'd placed on her temple...

"It seems silly to me, too," she told him in

a voice she wished hadn't come out sounding so breathy.

"So maybe you and I can just have our own little peace treaty," Dallas suggested.

"And who knows? Maybe it will have a ripple effect and our families will stop doing what they've always done."

"Oh, you really are an optimist, aren't you?" Dallas teased her.

Nina smiled but before she could say more a voice from the top of the stairs hollered, "Ready for inspection."

The challenging tone told Nina that it was Jake alerting Dallas that showers were finished, pajamas were on and whatever bedtime routine followed from there was ready to begin.

"I'll be up in a minute," Dallas called back. Then to Nina he said, "I don't make them line up and stand at attention or anything— I know that's how that sounds. But if I don't check, they've been known to turn on the shower, sit on the floor and look at a comic book, then turn the water off and figure I'll never know that they didn't bother to actually get in. And don't even get me started on the tooth brushing—"

"I understand," she said.

"It will only take me a minute, though, and I'll be right back."

He wanted her to wait, he wanted this evening to go on.

And so did Nina.

But it just didn't seem wise. She'd done what she'd intended to do—maybe more because there was a cheerier atmosphere to the house now that didn't have anything to do with the decorations—and having this little while on their own had just been a bonus. So she knew this was the moment it all had to come to an end.

"I should get going," she told him resolutely, setting her mug on the scarred coffee table and standing without any difficulty—something she was suddenly grateful that pregnancy hadn't robbed her of the way it did other women she'd seen at this stage.

"Let me at least walk you out, then," he said, sounding disappointed.

At the door, he helped her on with her coat then slipped into his on the way outside.

"I can't tell you how grateful I am for all this tonight," he said as they reached her SUV and he opened her door for her.

"It was my thanks to you," Nina reminded.

"But doing the work was enough. Total up

the cost of the tree and all that stuff and I'll come in and pay you."

Just the idea that he would come in to the store, that she would get to see him again, made that offer tempting to Nina.

But she shook her head. "Absolutely not. I just hope maybe this, tonight, helped you get more in the mood."

She meant in the *Christmas* mood but the way she'd said it had somehow managed to sound racy. And it made Dallas grin.

He had a great smile and an even greater grin.

And seeing it was payment enough for Nina.

Payment that sent goose bumps of delight up and down her arms…

How had any woman left a man like him behind? she wondered suddenly.

But merely having that thought jolted her slightly, and in response she got in behind the steering wheel, turning on the ignition to warm the engine before she glanced back at Dallas.

He was standing with his hand on the door, studying her, his grin now a small, thoughtful smile. And he was looking at her in a way that caused her to feel that same connection to him that she'd felt before. The connection that was personal and private, solely between them.

"This was really...good," he said as if labeling the evening *good* was an understatement but he couldn't think of how else to put it. "I enjoyed it," he added as if that surprised him.

"Me, too," Nina answered softly, unable to keep from admitting it herself.

Another moment passed while they stayed like that, as if Dallas couldn't quite let her go.

But then he took a step that put him out of the way of the door closing and said, "Drive safe."

"As a rule, I do," she joked in reference to the events of Wednesday.

That made his smile widen, but he didn't say anything else. He just closed her door, waved through the window and returned to his house as Nina made a U-turn and headed out the way she'd come in.

It was only as she drove back to Rust Creek Falls that she reminded herself that she was in no way on the market or in the market—or in the position or the shape—to be starting anything with any man.

Let alone Dallas Traub.

Chapter 4

By Wednesday evening it felt to Nina as if it had been decades since she'd seen Dallas, and she wondered what on earth was going on with her.

She couldn't stop thinking about the guy. She daydreamed about him. She dreamed about him in her sleep. She looked at every man who walked into the store, hoping it would be him. She found herself trying to come up with "accidental" ways to meet—as if driving out to the Triple T ranch and pretending her car engine had died right in front of his house would in any way appear to be an accident.

She was a little afraid that she'd lost her mind.

Before they were stranded together in that blizzard she had only been vaguely aware that he existed. And even then only as one of the group of hated Traubs. Individually he'd meant nothing to her. And now she woke up in the middle of the night vividly reliving being carried in his arms across that country road. Wishing he were there with her in her bed so he could put those same arms around her again, and convinced that she was truly going crazy.

She told herself that it was the flood of pregnancy hormones. That even though this was the worst time ever for her to be attracted to someone, maybe a sort of biological imperative had kicked in and caused it anyway, to tempt her to mate.

Or maybe she couldn't stop thinking about him as some sort of involuntary distraction mechanism to keep her from worrying about labor and delivery. Because she was definitely thinking more about Dallas than she was about going into labor.

About his gray-blue eyes and his distinctive nose and his crooked smile and his great hair and that body that just didn't quit...

But whatever was causing it, it was all torture. This was a man she had no reason to ever see again. A man she wasn't even very likely to run into, despite the size of Rust Creek Falls, because the conflict between their families had made it so that they occupied completely different parts of the town in order for their paths *not* to cross.

And yet he was the one man she was just dying *to* see.

It was crazy.

But she was hoping for some diversion, at least for tonight.

The flood that had hit Rust Creek Falls early in the summer had wreaked widespread havoc and destruction on much of the small town and the surrounding farms and ranches. It had cost the previous mayor his life and resulted in the election that had increased the animosity between the Crawfords and the Traubs. The damage to the elementary school had required it to be closed for repairs and classes so far this year to be held in the homes of the teachers of each grade.

Aid and relief efforts had helped. People in neighboring Thunder Canyon had done all they could. A New York–based organization called Bootstraps had become involved, and one of their volunteers, Lissa Roarke, had been particularly instrumental in bringing the needs of Rust Creek Falls to the attention of the rest of the country by appearing on a network talk show, as well as starting a charity website and blog that had brought in funds.

But many people were still struggling. And while the situation had improved and rebuilding was ongoing, full recovery would take time.

Many of the natives of Rust Creek Falls who had left the area to pursue careers and lives beyond the confines of a small town had returned to help, and the current residents who were lucky enough to have their homes and businesses spared—like the Crawfords—were determined to do all they could for the less fortunate among them.

One of those efforts on Nina's part was sponsoring and overseeing Santa's Workshop. She'd instigated the Tree of Hope—a Christmas tree in Crawford's General Store that had gone up in November. It was decorated with wish-list tags filled out by local children and families in need.

Donations of food, clothing and toys had been coming in to supply the "wishes" written on those tags, with the Crawfords committed to filling any gaps to make sure that everyone in Rust Creek Falls had gifts and a complete Christmas dinner this year, no matter what it took.

Organization of the donations had been ongoing, but with Christmas a week away, Nina had put signs in the store windows and all around town asking for volunteers to come to the store tonight to wrap packages and put food baskets together so that they could be delivered over the coming weekend. And that was what she was hoping would keep her mind off Dallas Traub for at least a few hours—gift wrapping and filling Christmas dinner baskets alongside any number of the good people of Rust Creek Falls whom she had faith would show up.

She'd asked her parents to take over the running of the store for the evening, and at six o'clock she opened the back door of the stockroom, where the necessary tasks were to be performed.

Already there were folks waiting to be let in, to get to the tables Nina had set up in the stockroom for work.

And when one of the volunteers proved to be Dallas, there was no containing her exhilaration, even though she tried.

"Hi!" she greeted him more brightly and

enthusiastically than she had anyone else. "I can't believe you came…"

He seemed slightly reserved and somewhat tentative but he still managed a joke.

"Was there fine print on the fliers that I missed that said 'No Traubs'?"

"No. I just… I'm so glad to see you. We can use all the help we can get," she said, stumbling over her words and settling on something she hoped hid what she was really thinking and feeling.

"Does my being here cause problems?" he asked, misinterpreting her nervousness. "Will it upset your family too much?"

"No, it's okay. My parents are out front, running the store. Nate is back here to keep things organized for easy loading on delivery day, but I have one table that's kind of back in a nook—you and I can wrap packages there and that shouldn't bother anyone."

"You're sure?" Dallas asked, more of that reserve showing than facing her family seemed to warrant.

"Absolutely positive. Come on, I'll show you," she encouraged, taking him to the very rear of the stockroom, where they could be secluded. "This was going to be my station, anyway. Unless you'd rather be somewhere else…"

"No! I mean, we've already established that you and I work well together. Why shouldn't we do it again? And it's probably better if I'm not right under your brother's nose," he said, doing some verbal tap dancing himself.

"Okay then," Nina concluded. "I put some of the smaller toys back here to wrap, since this space is limited. How are you as a gift wrapper?"

"Fair with paper, lousy with ribbons or bows."

"Then you do the paper, I'll do the ribbons and bows."

"Works for me," he said, with a little more excitement at what was in store for him.

He was wearing his heavy suede coat again and he took it off then. It had been on over jeans that were much nicer than what he'd worn Sunday night and a navy blue V-neck sweater with a white crew-necked T-shirt underneath.

A sweater that made his shoulders look even bigger and stronger...

Nina chastised herself for thinking that. It was just the sort of image that stayed in her mind to haunt her later and make it all the more difficult not to think about him.

"Paper station. Ribbons-and-bows station,"

she decreed, pointing to one end of the fold-out card table for him to go to and taking the opposite end herself to face him while she worked.

She had on maternity skinny jeans, this time with her most comfortable flat shoes and a boatneck, dark purple sweater long enough to fall well past her stomach.

"I can't say that I expected you to do this tonight," she said as they got busy.

"After Sunday? You earned a little pay-back," he said. "My brother Sutter wasn't busy, so he could babysit, and I get a night out—seemed like a win all the way around."

"This is a night out for you?" Nina laughed.

He grinned at her as if being with her was what mattered and said, "A good one."

Her brother came looking for her just then, and when he spotted Dallas his expression went from sweet to sour before he seemed to decide against whatever he'd been going to say and merely asked where she wanted the baskets stored.

"They can go into cold storage—I cleared enough space for them, and in there the tur-keys and hams will stay cool," she informed him, wishing he could be more congenial but knowing she was hoping for too much.

"Sorry," she whispered to Dallas when her brother had left.

"Hey, he didn't physically throw me out—I count that as a win," he said as if not even her brother's rudeness could upset him at that moment.

Still, it embarrassed Nina. And reminded her of just how complicated it was for a Crawford to have anything to do with a Traub.

And yet, not even knowing that could change how she felt about being right there, right then, with Dallas...

"Ah, this is *great!*"

The first thing that went through Nina's mind when Dallas said that was that he was talking about what she was thinking about—being with her in spite of the difficulties.

Then she realized he was getting ready to wrap an action figure that had sparked his interest and admiration, and seemed to have made him relax a bit.

"He turns into a fighter jet—my boys would all love this," he added.

It sounded as if Dad would, as well, and as Nina cut some wrapping paper for him to use she said, "And maybe if you're good, Santa will bring you one, too."

He laughed at her goad and played along.

"I'd *love* that! One of my favorite Christmas gifts was a robot that turned into a race car. When my younger brother Clay broke it there was war."

"Brother against brother?" Nina asked facetiously.

"Brother*s* against brother*s*—I had Forrest and Braden on my side—we were the oldest three and they had two of the other figures that went with mine so we were the Bad Guy Busters." He said it with dramatic effect before going on. "Clay had put a big dent in the game by breaking my guy. He enlisted Sutter and Collin—who I think might have been involved in breaking the toy in the first place because those three younger ones were always after our stuff—and it was all-out war. There were more toy casualties on both sides, a toilet head-dunking, rocks put in shoes as retaliation—"

Nina laughed. "How long did this particular civil war go on?"

"Oh, a full two days. Until Mom found sand in the younger boys' beds—that was the last straw. The Bad Guy Busters had its action figures confiscated, we all went without dessert for a week, the younger guys were sentenced to folding our socks that same week,

and Braden, Forrest and I had to *nicely* play
what we considered *baby* board games with
Clay, Collin and Sutter as our punishment."

"And peace was restored?"

"Until the next time," he said, as if it had
been a continuing saga. "We were six boys—
there were more battles than I can remember.
Weren't there in your house? You come from
a big family, too."

"The same as yours—six kids. And yeah,
there were plenty of fights. My sister, Natalie, and I would get into it. The boys would
get into it. Sometimes it was the girls against
the boys, or just Natalie or I would be fighting
for some reason with Nate or Brad or Jesse
or Justin. I've heard that only-children actually go into relationships at a disadvantage
because they haven't had the experience of
fighting with siblings."

Dallas laughed that deep barrel-chested
laugh he had. "Well then, my kids have that
advantage because they do their fair share of
fighting, too."

He handed her the wrapped package and
started on a baby doll while Nina tied the first
gift with ribbon and chose a bow.

"How about you?" he asked as she did.
"What was your favorite Christmas gift?"

"There was a doll the size of a real four-year-old that I wanted when I was about nine—I still have it tucked away to give to my own daughter if I have a girl, now or later. But I'd have to say that there was a tie between that as my favorite Christmas gift and a small television I lobbied for forever when I was thirteen. I wanted to be able to watch what *I* wanted to watch without having to negotiate with brothers or my sister or my parents, and I *loved* that."

"You wanted to do what you wanted to do whether anyone else liked it or not even then, huh?"

Nina laughed. "Pretty much."

"Yeah, having my own stereo was just as big a deal for me. My own stereo and a set of headphones so I could listen to what I wanted, as loud as I wanted."

"And what kind of music did you listen to?"

He told her and she couldn't resist giving him a hard time. "Oh, I get it—oldies."

"Hey!" he countered as if he was insulted. But his grin gave him away.

"To me, those were oldies," she said with a smile.

"I suppose they were," he conceded. "You're just a *baby* after all. A baby having a baby..."

Some goading of his own.

Nina laughed, enjoying herself. Enjoying him and this back-and-forth between them. "Well, at least the diapers *I'll* be buying won't be—"

"If you say for an adult I just might come across this table and—"

"Wave your cane at me?"

That made him laugh again. "It's a good thing I'm not sensitive. But be careful because I am a *spry* thirty-four and I could come over this table..."

He made that sound far more intriguing than threatening and she liked that he could poke fun at himself. Plus, for some reason what sprang into her mind was just how *spry* he'd been when he'd carried her across that country road in the blizzard. And as much as she wished their age difference produced something unattractive about him, it didn't. She couldn't deny that he was a very, very fine specimen of a man.

"So tell me what else you like besides controlling the television," he said then. "What toppings do you like on your pizza?"

"Is there a *bad* topping on a pizza?"

"Good answer!" he declared. "Sometimes you want it loaded with meat, sometimes peppers and onions and mushrooms and olives do just fine."

"Or just plain cheese or even white pizza—how can you go wrong with pizza?" Nina agreed. Then she said, "Ice cream—favorite flavor?"

"Again, no bad ice cream. I'm an ice cream guy...."

"Okay, let's narrow it down—chocolate or vanilla?"

"Chocolate. You?"

"Chocolate. The deepest, darkest, richest—"

"Chocolate," he finished for her with another grin. "Got it. How about movies? What's your favorite movie?"

They went on like that while they continued to work, and by the time all the packages were wrapped and the volunteers were beginning to leave, Nina had learned that she and Dallas Traub had a great deal in common. And that there still wasn't anything about him that she *didn't* like.

In fact, spending that time with him only made her like him more. Much to her dismay...

By ten-thirty the store had closed, Nate had left along with Nina's parents, and Nina was walking out the last of the volunteers. Except Dallas. She wasn't sure if she was misreading something, but it seemed as if he was hanging back, as if he wasn't eager to leave.

He was straightening up while she thanked her helpers. When she closed the stockroom's back door after they'd left she turned and leaned against it, weary from her fifteen-hour workday, but even so, not anxious to see Dallas go.

"Don't worry about taking the tables down. My stockers will do it in the morning when they come in," she said to Dallas as he finished folding one up.

"I don't mind," he said.

She shook her head. "No, you've done enough." As much as she didn't want this evening to end, she didn't have the heart to ask more of him.

Dallas checked the time on the wall clock above the time-stamp machine next to the door. "I suppose I should probably get going," he conceded. "Tomorrow is a school day, so I have to have the kids up at dawn."

He disappeared back into the alcove of shelves where they'd worked and reappeared with his coat, putting it on as he came to the door.

"It's nice that you just have to go upstairs and you're home," he observed.

"Really nice on days this long," she agreed. But she was still leaning against the closed door, essentially blocking his exit.

He didn't seem in any hurry, though, because when he joined her he sat gingerly on the table below the time-stamp machine where she kept new time cards and bulletins for her employees.

She also kept a bowl of buttermints there, just as a small treat for anyone who might want one coming or going. Dallas helped himself to a mint, squeezing it out of its packaging into his mouth.

"Thanks for coming tonight and all you did," Nina said as he ate it.

"The flood made this year rough. I was glad to see the names on those gifts—it's good to know that everyone, but especially the kids, won't be missing out on Christmas morning because of it. And you're doing food baskets, too?"

"There was a sign-up sheet. Some people put their own names on it, knowing they couldn't afford a real Christmas dinner this year. Some people put the names of friends or family or neighbors on it who they knew were too proud to do it themselves. I just hope everybody who needs it was brought to our attention one way or another. It's Christmas, after all. I want everybody to be able to sit down to a nice Christmas dinner."

He studied her, smiling, a warmth in his eyes that heated her to the core. "That's great..." he said softly, almost more to himself than to her. "And a lot of work," he added. "You must be tired."

Nina merely shrugged. "It's worth it."

"But you need some fun, too...." He hesitated, as if he wasn't sure what her response might be to what he was about to say. Then he came out with it anyway.

"Since you opened my eyes to my Scroogeness this year, I'm trying to be more conscious of making this a decent Christmas for the boys," he joked, making Nina laugh. "Friday night the snow castle opens and I promised I would take them. You wouldn't want to go with us, would you?"

The Montana town usually had enough snow by this time to inspire townsfolk to start using it for entertainment—there had been years when there were snowmen and snowwomen on every street corner; sometimes there was a snow-sculpting contest. One year there had been an entire snow fort. This December they'd erected a snow castle complete with a snow maze that led up to a cupola where Santa was to make an appearance on Friday night.

"I know the store is on Christmas hours, and maybe you have to work or something," he added into the miniscule pause left when Nina didn't answer immediately.

But she hadn't answered yet because her immediate desire was to say yes, and she'd forced herself not to jump in, to think about the complications and the reasons she should say no.

Unfortunately, when it came down to it, those complications and reasons just didn't carry enough weight against the drive to say yes.

"I actually don't have myself scheduled for the evening hours so I'm free..." she said, even though those complications and reasons didn't make that exactly true.

But everyone—including Nina—had been watching the castle being built in the past few days, and she wanted to go.

And she especially wanted to go with Dallas now that the opportunity had arisen, so she couldn't make herself turn him down.

Despite everything else...

"I'd love to go," she finished.

Dallas grinned at her answer. "Robbie is clinging to the last belief in Santa Claus, and this year, for some reason, he's really determined to talk to him."

"I think as long as kids believe you should let them."

"Me, too. I've warned his brothers not to bust his bubble, and they're being pretty good about it. Kids in his class have told him Santa isn't real, but he's just telling them they're wrong."

"Yeah, this is probably his last year," Nina said with a laugh. "But let him have it while he can."

"So you'll go?"

"I will," Nina said without any hesitation this time. "Unless the boys might object...?"

"Hey, after Sunday night they think *you're* Santa Claus. I've been fielding questions since then about when we're going to see you again, so they'll be thrilled."

"That's nice," Nina said, touched.

"You put the spirit in Christmas this year when I dropped the ball," he admitted. "And I have to say that it's helped to have a little cheer in the house.... It's helped me and the lousy mood I've been in for this last year—and I'm not even just keeping up appearances,

I'm actually feeling it. So, what do you say? Maybe around seven Friday night? We'll come by here and get you?"

What harm could come of it? Nina asked herself. She was pregnant and couldn't let anything romantic develop between them. And the three kids he already had would be there as chaperones.

It was just something to do. Something she wanted to do and otherwise probably wouldn't since she didn't yet have a child to take to see Santa.

"Seven works for me," she confirmed.

"Great!" he said with that slow, one-sided grin as he got up from the table.

Nina knew she couldn't go on holding him hostage by blocking the door, so she stepped away from it. But not so far away from it that she wasn't still standing there, facing him, when he reached for the handle.

"Thanks again for the help," she repeated.

"My pleasure," he assured her, his blue eyes holding her gaze.

And what flitted through her mind in that instant was the kiss he'd placed on her temple when they'd been stranded.

It was something she'd thought of more often than she wanted to admit since it happened, but there it was again—just a vague recollection of what it had felt like.

Accompanied by the inexplicable wish that he would kiss her again...

Though not on the temple.

On the lips.

And that it wouldn't be a kiss meant only to comfort her. It would be a real kiss....

Then she caught herself.

Thoughts—feelings—such as these weren't so harmless. And she shouldn't be having them.

She took a step away from Dallas, knowing that in the shadow of those thoughts of kissing, the wish that he would, she should tell him she'd just remembered something else she had to do on Friday night, so she couldn't go to the snow castle with him, after all.

But then he smiled at her again—this time a small, thoughtful smile—just before he opened the stockroom's back door and said, "Go on, get up to your place and relax. I'll see you Friday night."

And the only thing she heard herself say was, "Friday night."

Then he left, and she was flooded with disappointment.

Disappointment that he was gone.

Disappointment that he hadn't kissed her.

Disappointment that she knew she had no business having.

After a fifteen-hour workday at eight months pregnant—she was just tired, she told herself. That's why she felt what she did.

She hadn't honestly wanted Dallas Traub to kiss her.

But regardless of how she tried to believe it as she turned off the stockroom lights and went up to her apartment, she still took with her that disappointment.

And an awful, niggling curiosity that other kiss just hadn't satisfied.

About what it might be like to have Dallas Traub kiss her full on the mouth, for real…

Chapter 5

"Our snow guys went all out with this, didn't they?" Dallas marveled to Nina as they followed his three boys through the maze on Friday evening.

"It's beautiful, isn't it?" Nina agreed.

Dallas enjoyed the sight of her peeking through a cutout in the maze's wall to view one of many Christmas dioramas along the path of the maze.

There were also decorative carvings in the walls themselves, glittering with life from the glow of the tiny white Christmas lights overhead.

The castle at the end of the maze had been

carved from a wall of snow, and after crossing the drawbridge into it, Santa came into view. He was sitting on a red-velvet throne positioned on an ornately sculpted wooden platform.

"There he is!" Robbie exclaimed at first glimpse. "Are we in line?"

"I think we are, buddy," Dallas assured his son, since once they crossed the drawbridge there was a choice of going straight ahead to Santa or turning off and following what appeared to be portions of the maze that led back out.

"Are you gonna sit on Santa's lap?" Jake goaded him, nudging Ryder with an elbow.

"Jake…" Dallas said in a warning tone.

"Sure I am. That's how you talk to Santa," Robbie answered his brother, as if Jake were ignorant.

"You already wrote him a letter," Ryder said.

"This is different," Robbie insisted.

"Well, don't take too long. My nose is cold," Ryder grumbled, ducking his stocking-capped head deeper into the collar of his coat. His gloved hands were in his pockets and his posture was sulky now that they were at a standstill.

"Do this," Nina said, demonstrating by cupping her hands over her own mouth and nose and blowing warm breath into them.

Much to Dallas's relief, Ryder complied rather than answering her with more of his sullenness.

Dallas leaned over enough to say quietly into her ear, "I'm glad he spares you the preview of adolescence he gives me."

"You've taught him good manners," she whispered back, making him wonder how she always managed to make him feel better.

A moment later they reached Santa, just as the child on Santa's lap finished.

"Okay, Robbie, you're up," Dallas said. The smallest Traub marched purposefully to Santa and climbed onto his lap without hesitation. Nina and Dallas followed close behind, and the other boys stood off to the side.

Needing to know exactly what his son would be expecting from Santa, Dallas listened intently.

"I a'ready wrote down what I want on that letter I sent you," Robbie informed Santa matter-of-factly as he took a small photograph from his pocket. "But I need to give you this."

Dallas had no idea what Robbie was up to and paid even closer attention.

The little boy handed Santa the photograph. "It's my school picture. I don't know where my mom is but when you bring her presents this year, would you give her this, too? I think she might want it."

Boom! Dallas felt as if something had hit him. Hard. Just one more blow this year had to dish out to him when he least expected it....

He didn't know why, but he looked to Nina.

Only, she had tears in her eyes, and seeing that put him too close to panic, so he looked back to Robbie.

It just hadn't occurred to him that his son might have been so determined to see Santa because he was desperate to connect with the mother who wasn't around anymore, and for the life of him, Dallas wasn't sure what to do.

Should he break in and stop this? Should he let it go on?

Santa was equally at a loss, and looked to Dallas for guidance, so Dallas knew he had to figure something out fast.

Going on instinct, he went nearer and patted Robbie on the back. "I'm sure your mom will want it and be really glad you thought to get Santa to bring it to her." Then he nodded at Santa to take the picture.

"You think Santa knows where she is?" Ryder demanded bitterly.

Dallas heard the pain that went with that bitterness and it was another punch that he could only absorb before he cast his other son a warning look. It was Robbie who answered Ryder. "Santa knows where everybody is. How do you think he gives 'em presents?"

Ryder rolled his eyes, but Jake's eight-year-old tough-guy image seemed to have been shaken, and he looked as though he might be wondering whether his younger brother had come up with something he should have gotten in on.

Then Robbie hopped down off of Santa's lap and said, "Thank you, Santa. Tell my mom I've been a good boy this year, and I miss her."

"Merry Christmas!" Santa said, as he handed Robbie a candy cane—and two more for his brothers.

"Was that okay?" Robbie asked his father as they headed through the exit portion of the maze.

Dallas had to swallow a lump in his own throat before he could say, "Sure it was okay. It was nice. I'm proud of you for thinking of it."

Then he palmed Jake's head in one hand,

leaned over and said, "We can get your school picture and Ryder's, too, to Santa for the same thing, if you guys want."

"She can't have my picture," Ryder said angrily.

"Yeah, mine, either," Jake chimed in, the tough guy back in place, but not securely, and clearly to disguise his own hurt feelings.

Dallas glanced at Nina again, this time feeling the urge to rescue her, and apologized. "Sorry you had to get in on this...."

"It's okay. I know you all have to be struggling."

Her compassion and understanding caused him to like her even more, and he realized that somehow just having her there with him made this whole thing easier to bear.

They exited the maze just in time for the puppet show being done not far away, so they watched that. It seemed to help everyone recover because by the end of it the boys were all laughing, and that let Dallas relax again.

Then they moved on to watch a juggler being harassed by a mime before the boys all picked out Christmas ornaments to have their names engraved on and played various games that involved snowballs in one way or another.

Just when everyone was getting too cold to be out much longer, they encountered Dallas's brother Braden.

"Mom said this is where you were tonight, so I came looking for you." Braden greeted Dallas and gave a curious, confused glance at Nina, whom he obviously had not expected to find on the excursion.

Much to Dallas's further dismay, Braden ignored her and spoke only to him. "I want to get an early start in the morning, so I thought I'd take the boys to spend the night."

"Yeah!" Robbie agreed enthusiastically.

"Whenever you're done here," Braden added.

"I'm done. It's cold," Ryder contributed.

"Sure," Dallas agreed with a shrug.

Braden glanced at Nina again, his expression confused and disapproving. He still didn't acknowledge her, but he did seem to make a reluctant concession by saying to Dallas, "You don't have to end your night. I can just take the boys. I have my key, so we can swing by your place to get their stuff."

"Okay," Dallas answered, going on to sort through the details of what was going to be an ice-fishing trip for Braden and the boys the next day.

Then, after Dallas reminded the boys to say good-night to Nina and they complied, they left with their uncle. Without their uncle ever having said a word to Nina.

Dallas closed his eyes, letting his head drop forward and just hang for a moment as he dealt with the remnants of what had been dredged up in him tonight.

But as he told himself yet again to put a good face on things, even if he was still recovering from the body blows of the evening, it occurred to him that knowing he was going to open his eyes to Nina, knowing that he was about to have more time with her, left him genuinely feeling better. More than better, actually. It left him feeling glad to go on, despite everything else.

Then he took a deep breath and looked at her again, and smiled a smile that felt as if it was for her alone.

"Okay. Sometimes things just take a turn on you," he said. "First the deal with Santa and then my brother being rude—"

Nina laughed. "No more rude than my brother was to you the other night at the store," she pointed out.

Dallas shook his head. "Yeah. Wow. Coming at us from all directions. So, how about we salvage what we can of tonight, get out of this cold and get some hot wings?"

"Comfort food?" Nina said with a warm smile that had a power all on its own to raise him out of despair.

"Comfort food," he confirmed.

Then he linked his arm through hers and led her away from the event that had started out fun, hit a few snags but seemed as if it just might be salvageable after all.

"Will you be up all night with heartburn now?"

Nina laughed at Dallas's concern. She'd suggested they take their hot wings back to her apartment to eat because the restaurant had been so crowded. They'd finished the spicy snack and were throwing away the containers.

"I actually don't have a problem with heartburn, no matter what I eat. Or even what time of day I eat it," she answered, as they took their glasses of herbal iced tea with them into her living room.

"You're amazing—are you *sure* you're pregnant?"

She laughed again, glancing down at the long sweater she was wearing over leggings and boots. "I'd be dressed a little differently if I wasn't."

"Still hard to tell," he said.

"Take a drink of the herbal tea and think about the wine I would ordinarily have opened. Then tell me you aren't convinced."

He grinned at her, set his glass on the coffee table and pushed up the sleeves of the heavy crewneck T-shirt he was wearing.

His wrists were thick above those massive workman's hands, his forearms were impressively muscled and there was something so masculine about it all that it struck Nina as incredibly sexy.

She instantly chastised herself for that, also taking herself to task for liking what she saw as much as she did.

But she *did* like it. There was no denying it.

Pulling her eyes away, she decided to finally venture a question of her own. "Are you doing okay? I mean, it ripped my heart out to hear what Robbie said to Santa. I can't imagine that it was easy for you."

"Yeah, it pretty much ripped my heart out, too," he admitted. "I had no idea that was the reason he was so determined to talk to Santa this year. I guess it also explains why he still needed to hang on to believing Santa was real—he's been coming up with more reasons than you can imagine to convince us all, but I suppose he was really just trying to keep himself convinced."

"Do you think he feels like Santa is his only hope of reaching his mother?"

"I'm never too sure what's going on in any of the boys' heads. Sometimes they talk a little about what they're feeling, sometimes it comes out like this. But Laurel's family is all gone, her friends don't know where she is, so sure, I guess Robbie has to feel like Santa is his only hope," Dallas confided grimly. "And not only is that the sad truth, it's even sadder that Santa is no hope at all."

That fact, and the injury that showed in Dallas's expression, broke Nina's heart all over again. And even though she knew she was prying, her curiosity got the better of her so she did it anyway.

"You were married to Laurel Hanes, weren't you?"

Dallas grimaced, bent his head forward and rubbed the back of his neck as if to ease some stress there. "Yeah," he acknowledged as he raised it back up again. "For nine years. But we were together for twenty—from the time we were both thirteen."

So he'd spent most of his life with the woman, and whittling it down to only the marriage seemed to diminish it somehow.

"Childhood sweethearts," Nina said to validate the time he'd spent with his ex. "But you didn't get married until you were twenty-four?"

"Not because of me. I would have married her right after high school. But Laurel dragged her feet. 'Marriage is forever, why rush it?' That's what she'd say. She wanted to stretch her wings a little. To travel some with her friends. To just have fun before we settled down. I didn't have any doubt that we'd get there—no one did, it just always seemed like a given that Laurel and I would be together forever—so I didn't push it. I just weathered my mom pressuring me for a wedding and grandchildren—the sooner the better, in her point of view—and waited for Laurel to be ready."

"I'm sure Laurel appreciated your patience," Nina said when his tone let her know he now considered that somehow foolhardy.

"That sounds good but I just think I was too dumb to see the forest for the trees," he muttered.

"But she was eventually ready," Nina pointed out.

Dallas made a face at that. "Not exactly. Laurel got pregnant with Ryder."

And his expression told her that hadn't been such a joyous surprise.

"It was an accident," he added. "Laurel had the flu, missed a couple of birth control pills, and I guess we didn't take that seriously enough."

"Were you both unhappy about it?"

"I wasn't unhappy about it at all. By then it seemed like Laurel had had plenty of fun, plenty of wing-stretching. She'd done her traveling—her friends were actually all married and settled down themselves—so it seemed like our time to tie the knot. I just figured the baby was a sign for us to finally do it."

"And what did Laurel think?"

"It still took some convincing," he admitted. "But she came around."

"No enthusiasm? No running into your arms and saying 'Yes! I'd love to marry you and have this baby'?" Nina asked, thinking that that was the kind of response he'd deserved. The kind of response the coming of Ryder had deserved.

He chuckled wryly, humorlessly. "No, there was none of that. It was more like, 'Okay, I guess we have to....'"

"But once you actually got her to take the leap?" Nina was hoping for anything positive, for his sake.

"She didn't get any happier about it," he said reluctantly. "There were some times that were better than others," he claimed, as if to make it sound better. "She liked all the attention and parties and showers that came with the wedding and then with being pregnant, too. But after Ryder was born, the day-to-day got her down, and she just wasn't happy. She was restless and she complained that she was bored. Well, she pretty much complained about everything."

"But she didn't want out...." Nina said, because it was the most encouraging thing she could come up with.

"Like a divorce? No, she didn't talk about that. And if she thought about it... I don't know if she did, but *if* she did the idea probably got further and further away when her dad died, and then her mother a year later. That left her without any family, other than us."

"And I'm sure she loved you and the boys," Nina insisted, wanting to believe it herself.

"I suppose. In her own way. And she knew how it was with me, with my family—we believe in marriage. In marriage being for life. She knew that to me—to my family—divorce would be a disappointment, so I would have fought tooth and nail to keep that from happening."

There was such sadness, such shame in his tone that it was obvious the end of his marriage *had* left him feeling like a failure, seeing himself as a failure. Nina could only hope his family hadn't added to that, but her own lifelong prejudice against the Traubs left her thinking they might have.

"So, no talk of divorce and you had two more kids…." Nina said to prompt him to go on, wanting to understand.

"I talked her into Jake. I thought since she'd liked being pregnant, liked all the attention, maybe that might perk her up."

"And she agreed."

"Yeah. Plus…" He shrugged. "You know, she grew up the same way I did—probably the same way you did—believing that that's what people do, they get married, they have a family. I guess then she was sort of resigned to her lot in life."

"But having Jake didn't help?"

"No. And Robbie was another accident. She didn't actually want to go through with having him."

"She didn't want Robbie?" Nina asked defensively. It was painful to hear that the little boy who loved his mother so much hadn't been wanted by that mother.

Dallas confirmed it with another shrug. "I had to promise her a trip to Europe to get her to have him, and Laurel spent the whole nine months planning the holiday rather than planning anything for the new baby. Rather than even talking about the new baby. I think if we hadn't already had a crib and bottles and blankets and all the gear, she might have wrapped him in a bath towel, stuck him in a dresser drawer and called it good."

"So she probably wasn't any happier once her European vacation was over." Nina knew the minute she said the words that she shouldn't have let so much of her disapproval into her voice.

Dallas didn't seem to take offense, though. He merely shook his head. "Nope, no happier. In fact, I think the trip only made things worse. Coming back to her life here, to the day-to-day grind of just being a wife and mother, was a letdown."

Nina hadn't known Laurel Hanes, but she was growing to dislike her. "Did she consider a career? Hobbies? If her friends had kids, didn't she like doing things with them? She actually sounds depressed—did you think about going with her for counseling?"

"She didn't want to work, and since we didn't need the money I didn't push that. She tried hobbies—hated them all. When it came to her friends, she started saying that all they could talk about was their kids and cooking and this town, and she hated that, too. Yes, I did try to get her to talk to a doctor or a counselor—to *somebody*—but she wouldn't do it. She said *she* wasn't depressed, that everything around her was just depressing—if that makes any sense. It didn't to me."

"So there was, what? Five more years after Robbie was born?"

"Yep. Five more years. Then, the day after Christmas last year I woke up alone in bed. There was a letter from Laurel on her pillow. She said I'd been a good husband—better than her friends' husbands—that I'd made a good home for her, that I was a good father, but that she'd been sleeping with one of our itinerant ranch hands—"

"Oh, no…" Nina muttered, seeing the lines

of tension in his handsome face and knowing how hard that had struck him. How hard it would strike anyone. "Did you have any idea?"

"None. The ranch is a big place and I'm out on it from dawn till dusk most days. Robbie was in preschool, Ryder and Jake were at school, she was alone in the house, and the house isn't within sight of neighbors. I don't know for sure, because she didn't say in her note, but I give my ranch hands their jobs for the day and send them out to do them—I'm not watching them all the time. There's no way I could. I suppose that gave the guy free rein to drop by my place while I was out and..."

Seeing his anguish, his embarrassment, broke Nina's heart for the third time that night.

"I hauled that bed out to the middle of nowhere and set it on fire, I'll tell you that," he said under his breath. "I'd have set the whole damn house on fire if I could have, but about all I could do was gut the master bedroom and bath and redo it all with a vengeance."

Nina nodded. She could appreciate that he wouldn't have wanted the room where his wife had likely cheated on him to hold any reminders.

"Did the letter say anything else? Anything about the kids she was leaving behind?" Nina asked.

"It said that by the time I read it, Laurel and Jeff would be long gone from Rust Creek Falls. That, to her, living here was barely existing and that she needed to go out and live life. That there were divorce papers on the bureau that she'd had a lawyer draw up. That she didn't want anything but her freedom, she was giving me full and unconditional custody of the boys, and all I had to do was sign the papers and have them filed, and we could pretend none of it had ever happened."

Twenty years with someone, a marriage, a life, three kids and the woman wanted to pretend none of it had ever happened? Nina tried to hide the outrage she felt on Dallas's behalf.

"There wasn't so much as a clue where she went from here," he went on. "Not another word about the boys or a message to them, and we haven't heard from her since. As if nothing here exists for her anymore."

"She hasn't even called to see if the boys are all right or anything?"

He shook his head once more. "Nothing."

"Oh, Dallas, I'm so sorry," Nina told him, sorry not only for what had happened but also for the unkind thoughts she'd had about him when she'd heard a Traub was getting divorced. And now she knew why there wasn't any general knowledge of what had actually happened to end his marriage, that his wife cheating on him and running out on him with a ranch hand wouldn't have been something he'd wanted spread around.

He shrugged yet again. "In some ways we're better off," he said. "Laurel just never grew up and settled down, so she was like living with a sourpuss teenager—to the boys, too. She didn't have any patience with them. They annoyed and irritated her and she let them know it. She was just generally hard on them and she never really seemed to enjoy anything about them or with them—not even holidays or birthdays—"

"But she was still their mom, and to them—"

"Yeah, they lost their mother—I see that. But I'm hoping that when they're grown and they look back on things, they might remember the fits and rants Laurel threw. The broken dishes when she was mad for no good reason. Her stomping on toys and breaking them if they weren't put away when she wanted them put away. All her griping and complaining and screaming that she hated her life and all of us along with it. Her saying that Rust Creek Falls was worse than living in hell…"

Nina also took offense to that opinion of her hometown, the hometown that everyone was working so hard to rebuild. But she didn't say it. Instead she said, "I guess not everyone is cut out for living in a place like Rust Creek—I know I've seen my share of people who can't wait to get out."

"Yeah. Sure," he agreed. "But for me… I love it here—even though it does hold way too many memories of Laurel."

"I love it here, too," Nina chimed in. "I can't imagine ever living anywhere else. Or a better place to raise kids."

"If we can just get it back on its feet…"

"It's coming along," Nina said, knowing he was changing the subject.

She could tell he thought he might have said too much about his ex-wife and the problems they'd had, and that he wanted to rein that in some. And since getting off the subject softened his expression, Nina also thought it better to put the conversation to rest.

Besides, he was looking at her with eyes that were no longer clouded by anger or frustration or hurt when they stopped talking about his marriage, and that was nice. Eyes that were warm and full of something else entirely, and it made her melt a little inside...

Then he seemed to snap out of that, too, and maybe remember himself because all of a sudden he said, "Could the Traubs and their sordid history have dragged this night down any worse?"

Oddly enough, Nina realized that she wouldn't have traded a moment of it for anything. But she didn't quite know how to say that when her time with him and his boys had seen some pain for them all.

So she just said, "It wasn't so bad. It was better than a lot of Friday nights I've spent."

"Now you're just being nice," he said as if he appreciated it nonetheless. "But I should probably get going—I've boo-hooed us right into a late night."

He stood then. "Speaking of getting Rust Creek Falls back on its feet, though—you're delivering the toys and food baskets tomorrow, right?"

There had been talk of that on Wednesday night during the compiling of the baskets and the wrapping of the gifts, so it came as no surprise that he knew it.

"I am," Nina confirmed, standing, too.

"Well, the boys will be ice fishing all morning and then my folks are taking them into Kalispell to do some shopping, to have dinner and see a Christmas movie, so I'm on my own and I'd like to help."

"Deliver toys and baskets?"

"You. I'd like to help *you* deliver toys and baskets."

As much as it heated her up a few more degrees to hear that, it also set off an alarm in her. She liked this guy more and more with every minute they spent together, and that just shouldn't be happening. Now, of all times, she should be totally focused on the coming of her baby, on preparing for bringing her baby home, on her own future as a single parent. She should not be focusing on a man.

But it would be nice to have help tomorrow...

"I was thinking," he went on, "that my going along would also give me a chance to see what's happening with some of the still-struggling folks around here. I'd like to make sure they aren't being overlooked by the reconstruction teams."

She could hardly say no to that, could she?

Instead she said, "Okay..."

"Just tell me when you were planning to start, I'll come over and load the back of my truck, and we'll do some early Christmas giving."

Nina told him the time as he put his coat back on and they headed for her apartment door.

When they'd reached it, Dallas turned that lopsided smile to her and said, "Still no heartburn?"

Nina laughed. "None. You?"

"Threatening," he admitted, making her laugh even more.

"You know what they say about your thirties—your digestion slows down," she teased him.

He laughed. "I don't think anybody says that. And it's more likely caused by you getting the damned hottest wings that place sells."

She pointed to herself. "Not thirty, no heartburn." Then to him. "Over thirty, heartburn." Then she shrugged as if she'd proven her point.

He laughed again. "You know, you're just a little bit evil."

"As long as it's just a little bit…"

"Yeah, I wouldn't have it any other way," he confessed.

Then there it was—Nina was thinking about him kissing her again. Out of the blue. For no rational reason. Involuntarily.

Ahh, this is crazy, she lamented.

But it was still there.

Enough so that she felt her chin tip up to him, her eyes look more deeply into his, her lips part…

Stop, stop, a voice in her head shouted.

But he was coming closer. Bending slightly. Aiming…

He was going to do it. He was going to kiss her! And, oh, but she wanted him to!

Then he kissed her all right.

But he detoured and landed one on the tip of her nose.

And it wasn't enough.

It just wasn't.

She tilted her chin higher still and she kissed him.

Barely.

Briefly.

A mere brush of her lips to his. Not actually enough to give her more than a hint of what a real kiss from him might be, but still, she kissed him.

And then she looked into those blue eyes and noticed that his eyebrows were not arched high.

But he didn't say anything. He just smiled a very slow smile as he straightened up and said, "I'll see you around eight tomorrow morning to load up and we'll get on the road by nine."

Nina could only nod and say good-night before he left.

Before he left her to the voice in her head shrieking, *I kissed him! I kissed him!*

Then she told herself in no uncertain terms that a person who was eight-plus months pregnant had no business going around kissing men. Especially not Traubs.

But despite that, she was having trouble regretting it.

And she couldn't help wishing she'd done a better job of it when she'd had the chance…

Chapter 6

"Is this perfect timing or what? Breakfast!" Dallas said when he went in the back door of his parents' house at seven o'clock on Saturday morning.

"Ellie Traub, you're a saint," he added, setting the bag he'd brought in on the floor and taking off his coat to hang on a hook behind the door before leaning over to give his mother a peck on the cheek.

She was standing at the counter, coffeepot in hand. That greeting and the impromptu kiss he didn't ordinarily bestow had stalled her midpour. "Aren't you chipper this morning," she marveled.

"Sun's out melting the snow, the sky is as clear a blue as you could want, the air is crisp—it's a beautiful day."

His father's head pivoted slowly in his direction. Bob Traub took off his reading glasses, set down his newspaper and stared at his son.

"And I'm starving and that bacon smells fantastic!" Dallas announced.

His mother finished pouring coffee and reached into the cupboard for another cup for Dallas.

"There's not only bacon, there's sausage, scrambled eggs, hash browns, and toast and jam, too," she informed him, listing what was already prepared and piled on platters in the center of the kitchen table. "You're lucky there's anything left—Braden and your boys were already here to eat before they went out to the lake."

There was still plenty left. Having raised six sons, Ellie Traub had long ago gotten into the habit of cooking enough to feed an army.

Dallas took the chair he'd sat in at every meal growing up, joining his father while his mother got him a plate, napkin and silverware, and served him that steaming cup of coffee.

"There's cheese and peppers in the eggs, and

hot sauce if you want it," his mother said as she sat down across from him, watching him.

The mention of hot sauce reminded him of Nina and the hot wings and the night before. And the fact that she'd kissed him...

"Eggs and hot sauce make you happy?" his mom asked, sounding puzzled.

Dallas hadn't realized that he was smiling until that moment. But he couldn't seem to stop it. Not with the thought that in an hour he was going to be with Nina again. All day long.

"It's nothing," he answered, heaping food on his plate.

He ate heartily, complimenting his mother's cooking and his father's new choice of chicken feed for producing an improvement in the flavor of the eggs.

"And this coffee," he said after a sip of it. "Is there something different about it? It's great!"

"Same coffee, made the same way," his mother informed him, watching him even more intently.

"Jam's your mother's, though," his father said. "Delicious even though we had to use Colorado peaches because the flood did so much damage to the fruit trees around here."

Taking his father's comment as a recommendation, Dallas slathered the homemade peach jam on his toast, nodding as he did at the grocery sack near the door. "There's that change of clothes you wanted for the boys, Mom. Shoes, too. You're thinking that they'll be back from fishing around noon and you'll head for Kalispell?"

"If they make it until noon," his father piped up. "Last time I took those boys out on the ice the cold got to them after a couple of hours, and we had to come back. I'm betting they'll be here by ten and we'll be having lunch in Kalispell."

"The drive should be good, though. No bad weather on the horizon. A really, really beautiful day!" Dallas said.

"Chipper," his mother said to his father. "He's chipper."

Bob Traub shrugged. "He's in a good mood."

"For the first time in a year. He's been down-in-the-mouth and mopey, and none of us could get him out of it, and now, all of a sudden—"

"I'm sitting right here and the two of you are talking about me as if I'm invisible," Dallas said with a laugh.

Neither of his parents commented. Instead, his mother looked at him again and said, "What are your plans for today and tonight, with the boys off your hands?"

A dicey question. He considered lying. But he was a grown man, and it was his own business how he spent his time.

Besides, it was likely that word would get back to them about what he was actually going to do today, and he'd just get caught.

"Thought I'd help deliver the Christmas gifts and food baskets going out from that Santa's Workshop deal," he said as if there wasn't any Crawford connection.

But both of his parents paused their breakfasts to look at him as if he'd just grown gills.

"That's that thing coming from Crawford's General Store," his mother said. "Where you went the other night to help wrap presents…"

"Yep."

Then from his father, "Braden said that Crawford girl was with you and the boys last night."

"*Nina*—the boys knew her by name. Said they've been to her house…" his mother added.

"They've been to her *apartment*—she lives over the store. She wanted to thank me for that whole blizzard mishap."

Dallas saw one of his mother's eyebrows raise. "She's the pregnant Crawford, isn't she?" Ellie Traub said with a note of alarm in her voice.

Dallas had finished eating and sat back with his hand around his coffee cup. He knew all the negatives. Nina was a Crawford. She was pregnant. She was only twenty-five. Top all of that off with the fact that he had three kids, was still stinging some from Laurel leaving him and that he'd spent the past year just about as down on marriage and relationships and women in general as anyone could be, and there was nothing about what was happening with Nina that made any sense.

And yet...

He just couldn't seem to help himself. He couldn't seem to force himself to stay away from her. She made him feel good. And it was such a relief after the past year of feeling rotten....

"Yes, Nina is the pregnant Crawford," he answered his mother's question belatedly. And more somberly than anything he'd said since coming in the back door.

"Is she the reason you're in a better mood?" his mother persisted, sounding even more alarmed.

"The boys were cheerier, too, now that I think about it," his father observed before Dallas had a chance to answer.

"Because of *her?*" Ellie Traub demanded.

Dallas understood where the outrage in his mother's tone was coming from. She'd gone to great lengths to make things as normal and upbeat as possible for her grandsons since Laurel had disappeared, to do everything she could to make them happy. Of course it would hurt Ellie's feelings if she thought someone else had been more successful at it, let alone a Crawford.

And addressing that gave Dallas a way of avoiding the subject of whether or not Nina was responsible for his own lighter spirits.

"The boys are just looking forward to Christmas and being out of school for winter break after this week. And you're doing things like taking them to Kalispell today—that's what's making them cheerier."

"But you? Is that Crawford girl the reason you're in a better mood?" his mother demanded.

"Maybe it's just time passing," Bob Traub suggested to his wife.

But Dallas decided in that moment that he wasn't going to mislead them so he said, "I know Nina is a Crawford and around here the Crawfords are the enemy. But… I don't know…there's nothing wrong with her that I can see. She's a decent, kind, warm—"

"You like her," his mother accused him.

But, Dallas noted, with shock rather than rancor suddenly.

And so he admitted more than he even wanted to admit to himself.

"I do like her. She's a nice person."

"That's it? That's all there is to it?" his father asked hopefully.

"That's it," Dallas said because that *needed* to be all that was going on with Nina. "And she's doing a good thing with this Santa's Workshop deal, so I wanted to help out. Her friends and neighbors are our friends and neighbors, too, and making sure they have Christmas this year is important, no matter what."

He knew his parents agreed, and that was why they had nothing to say to it.

But after a moment his father said, "That girl *is* a Crawford though…"

"And an unwed mother," Ellie Traub cautioned.

Dallas sighed. "And if I don't take off I'm going to be late," he said, standing and taking his dishes to the sink.

As he got into his coat, he thanked them in advance for the boys' outing to Kalispell and told them to drive safely, that he'd be waiting when they got home this evening.

But it was really the time between now and then that he was thinking about. That he was looking forward to. The time he was about to spend with Nina.

Nina had not been excited by the prospect of delivering the food baskets and Santa's Workshop gifts. She hated that the flood had left so much need for the community and she was dreading seeing people she knew and liked still struggling in the aftermath. Especially at this time of year.

But sharing the chore with Dallas made all the difference. And not just because he did all the heavy work.

He approached each household like a friend making any ordinary Christmas visit to say hello and drop off a holiday token of that friendship. There was no air of charity to any of it—that was something Nina had set out to do, and she appreciated that Dallas offered that same attitude. But in the process he still managed to glean important information about how people were faring.

While Nina mostly chatted with the women of the households to learn their viewpoints and continuing difficulties, Dallas ended up on many tours that exhibited what progress—or lack of progress—had been made on houses or outlying properties. And several times Nina heard him make promises of his own services or resources after the holidays.

Together they came away with a lengthy list to pass along to the reconstruction crews and the other recovery efforts for special attention to things that were being overlooked or for additional needs that should be met. They made a good team—that was what occurred to Nina as the day progressed.

A good team. A twosome.

But not a couple—that was something that she had to keep reminding herself. They were *not* a couple.

Even though that was how it felt as they spent the day driving around together, chatting, comparing notes, sharing snacks—some that Nina hand-fed to Dallas as he drove—and then stopping to pay their joint visits.

It also struck her that in her entire four years with Leo she'd never had a day quite like that one and never felt as connected and as couplish as she did with Dallas.

But regardless of how it seemed—or felt—to her, they were not a couple.

A good team, yes—something else she'd never experienced with Leo.

A twosome—only for the day.

But not a couple.

Even if she had kissed him the night before.

Which she was determined should—and would—never happen again.

It was after seven that evening before the last of the baskets and gifts were delivered. As they headed back to the General Store and Nina's apartment, Dallas said, "That was a long day."

"It was," Nina agreed, sounding as weary as she felt. Ordinarily she had energy to spare, but she'd spent most of the previous night awake, worrying about that kiss even as she relived it again and again. So she was running on about four hours of sleep.

"I'm not much of a cook," he said conversationally, making her think of the TV dinners she'd seen at his place when she'd brought the Christmas tree. "But I do have one specialty—chicken in a butter and lemon sauce that I serve over linguine. Could I interest you in that for dinner tonight?"

"You want to cook me dinner?" Nina asked tentatively, unsure if he was serious.

"I do," he said firmly. "I'd like to fix you dinner, share it with you, then clean up the mess—all while you sit with your feet up, a beverage of your choice in hand and watch without lifting a finger."

"You'd *like* to do all that," she said dubiously, ignoring how wonderful it sounded to her. "Why, when you've just had as long a day as I've had?"

"Because all I've seen you do since the blizzard is work your little tail off, and today topped everything. I keep wondering when you get to be pampered. You do so much for everyone else, despite being pregnant—even though you don't look it—and it seems to me that there should be someone else doing something for you every now and then. And tonight I'd like it if you'd let it be me."

"Really?" Had her worries overnight that he might have hated her kissing him been for naught?

"Really. Play Cleopatra on the Throne and let me pamper you tonight."

"I don't have anything in gold lamé," she warned, telling herself to say no to this, to let today end now, but incapable of finding one whit of willpower to actually do that.

"I just want you comfortable. You can wear your bathrobe if you want."

"To a fancy dinner made just for me? Never!"

He cast her a half grin. "I didn't promise fancy, just chicken and linguine."

Nina laughed at him. "Okay. It sounds good," she conceded.

He pulled into a parking spot behind the store, near the back stairs to the outside entrance of her apartment, and turned off the truck engine.

"Then you go upstairs while I go shopping downstairs, and we'll do this," he instructed.

But that's all they'd be doing, Nina silently told herself. A simple dinner. Between people who were maybe becoming friends instead of enemies.

But nothing more than friends.

Friends who didn't kiss each other goodnight...

"Okay, enough! Your dinner was delicious, my kitchen is spotless, now come and sit down—you're making me feel guilty," Nina insisted an hour and a half later when Dallas had accomplished all he'd set out to do for her.

He put one final touch into polishing her faucet then folded the dish towel he'd used, set it on the counter and swept an arm in the direction of her living room so she would lead the way.

Nina did, going to sit on one end of her couch, facing the center of it with her feet tucked under her.

Dallas sat more toward the center, angled in her direction and stretching a long arm across the top of the back cushion to more or less face her. "I can't believe I forgot dessert," he lamented for the third time since he'd realized his oversight.

"I'm glad you did—I'm stuffed and you've already spoiled me rotten."

"Someone should," he said.

"Oh, absolutely. I'm all for it," she joked.

"I'm serious."

She could tell that he was, too—it was reflected in his expression. But he was so ruggedly gorgeous; the stern, stoic lines on his face only accentuated it and made Nina smile.

Undaunted, he went on anyway. "You should have some help this late in the game and then a lot more once you bring the baby home. Aren't there parts of doing this on your own that are a little tough on you?"

Nina shrugged. "My family helps where they can, and I know I can always call if I need more."

"That's not the same as having a husband or the father of the baby to lean on day-to-day."

"Having a husband or the father of the baby around wouldn't guarantee that I'd have someone to help," Nina insisted. "I know for a fact that Leo wouldn't have, even if the baby was his."

The lines on Dallas's face deepened into a frown. "Like I said during the blizzard, I knew Leo, but just as a guy who worked for us here and there. I didn't really *know* him. You thought he was a waste of time…"

"My time *with* him was wasted," she amended. "After four years of *somedays* that never came."

"Somedays?"

"Whenever I'd ask if we were headed for marriage, for having a family, he'd say, 'Sure, someday…'"

"But he was just leading you on?"

"I don't know. I'd like to believe that he at least thought he meant it when he said it. Otherwise it sort of makes me a dumb sap for having believed him, and it's bad enough that I came away from that whole time with him feeling like… I don't know, like his minion…"

That made Dallas smile. "His *minion?*"

"Well, I did pretty much do his bidding."

"Ohh, that doesn't sound good."

"Leo was ten years older and that put me at

a disadvantage. Especially the longer we were together. Leo was a creature of habit… I guess maybe we all tend toward that, but he loved to say he was set in his ways, that he needed his *routines,* that he'd been doing things the way he'd been doing them for years and years and couldn't change, that because I was so much younger I could be more flexible—"

"He's about the same age I am," Dallas said defensively, as if the other man's point of view didn't make sense to him.

But to Nina the fact that Dallas and Leo were about the same age was still noteworthy and she reminded herself not to lose sight of that.

"I have never said I'm set in my ways," Dallas claimed.

"But I'm sure you have habits, routines, things you've been doing the way you want to do them for years and years," Nina pushed.

"Sure, but like *you* just said, everybody does," Dallas countered.

"And everybody wants them to be adapted to, and with Leo, our age difference meant that—"

"He got his way and you didn't."

"Yes," Nina confirmed because that *was* what it had boiled down to.

"And you attribute that to him being a lot older than you are…"

"I loved him, and it just did seem easier for me to adapt to him. To him it was a big deal if we ate where and what and when he wanted to eat because if we didn't he didn't feel well. If I pushed him to do something I wanted to do, and he didn't enjoy it, he was cranky, he complained, and I didn't end up enjoying it, either. If he wanted to stay in and I made him go out there was yawning and moaning, and there was no telling where he might fall asleep—he actually did that in his chair at the table during a dinner party with one of my friends—"

"Wow. He really made sure it was all on his terms. So you just, what? Put whatever you wanted—or needed—on the back burner?"

"For the most part it wasn't a big deal to me—*for* me—to adapt. Especially when he just…couldn't. And I kept telling myself that it was all only small stuff, anyway. If he came home from work tired and I didn't…well, I was a lot younger, I had more energy, more stamina, I figured when I was ten years older I'd probably feel the same way—"

"So you took care of him."

"And I tried not to pressure him. It wasn't

as if I could *force* him to be younger and have more energy or stamina. Or if he had to eat what and when he had to eat, so what? But I made it clear that I wanted to get married, to have kids—"

"And that was where the *somedays* came in."

"Right."

"And when you pushed for that? Is that what ended the relationship?"

"I suppose you could say that was when *my* age became an issue. When I reached the time when I'd planned to start a family I told him so—"

"But *someday* still hadn't come for him?"

"No, he finally didn't just put me off—I suppose I should give him credit for that. He said that the more he thought about, the more he thought he just wasn't cut out for marriage and kids. He loved me and all—that's what he said—and it wasn't me. He said that he was perfectly happy going on the way we had been. But marriage and family just weren't for him."

"Did he think you might accept that?" Dallas asked, as if he thought the other guy was deluded.

"There was a part of him that seemed to…

I don't know…hold out hope for it, maybe. Because he tried to talk me into going on the way we had been. But I wouldn't." Nina stated the simple fact. "It was one thing to eat a hamburger at five when I might have wanted pizza at seven, or to watch an action movie when I would rather have seen the romantic comedy. But when it came to getting married, to having a baby… Well, that was my life we were talking about."

"It was time to draw the line," Dallas concluded, his tone compassionate and sympathetic, making it clear that he understood that it hadn't been as easy for her as it might sound.

"Yes," Nina confirmed quietly, more emotion creeping into her voice than she'd allowed before. But it *hadn't* been easy to accept that *someday* was never going to come with Leo. That she could either have Leo or the life she'd always wanted, but that she couldn't have them both. That those four years had been squandered with him.

It hadn't been easy to open her eyes and realize that she had to make a choice between postponing the family she wanted until she found someone else—all the while running the risk that she might not find someone else—or having that family on her own. Without anyone to help out with the day-to-day or to pamper her the way Dallas had tonight...

"So, that was it?" Dallas asked, interrupting her thoughts both with his words and by raising his hand from the top of the sofa back and using an index finger to gently follow the curve of the side of her face. "You ended it with Leo?"

"I did."

"I'm thinking that he might not have taken it too well, since he left town—which is a really big change for someone *set in his ways.*"

"My ending things actually did seem to shock him."

Dallas's smile was lazy and kind. "Well, you had set a precedent of giving him his way."

"I know. I had. I guess I just thought that we'd eventually end up on the same page—"

"That *someday* would come."

"Right. That, given time, he'd *want* to marry me. He'd *want* to have kids with me. Instead, the longer things went on and the older he'd gotten, the further he'd also gotten away from marriage and wanting to become a father." She shrugged again. "I didn't really see until then just how much the age difference put us at different places in our lives, which was a much bigger thing than just not being on the same page. For Leo, the ship had just sailed on a time to get married and start having kids, and I couldn't change that—"

"Any more than you could give him more energy or stamina."

Nina shrugged yet again. "Age *does* make a difference. Look at you and me—you have *three* kids. You're done with the baby stuff, you're on to the kids-in-school stuff. I haven't even changed my first diaper and you're probably thinking that you're glad never to change another one."

Dallas chuckled but didn't deny it.

Which cemented Nina's feelings that she had to be very careful not to get in too deep with yet another man at a stage of life different than her own.

"So no. If this was Leo's baby? I'd still be having to adapt to Leo," Nina concluded, ending where they'd begun this conversation.

"Yeah, but I'm still not sure that, with Leo, that wasn't as much an age issue as a personality issue," Dallas postulated.

"Sure, that had to be a part of it, too—lots of people, men and women, don't get married or start families until they're in their thirties. Or later. But still..."

But still, she also knew that a big age difference couldn't be discounted, that more years brought with them more baggage and deeper roots—like Dallas's own long-term history with his ex-wife and the scars left by the end of it, and the children who also now had to be a factor. Or her own child who would become a consideration she hadn't had before.

"But still, age is an issue," Dallas finished for her when she stalled. "Getting married and having kids at her age made Laurel feel as if she'd missed out on too much. Age plays a role, in one way or another, with us all, whether we like it or not."

"It just does..."

"And so for you and Leo, that was it? You ended things with him at a time when you wanted to start your family and you just went for it." He nodded in the direction of her bulging middle.

"Yep," she confirmed.

"On your own..."

"Yep."

He nodded his head slowly, acceptingly, without any indication of disapproval that she could see.

Then he said, "That takes a lot of courage. I gotta say, I admire it. And you're one hell of a lesson to me."

Nina laughed. "Are you telling me that the young pup is teaching the old dog new tricks?" she teased good-naturedly.

"Yeah," he said, laughing, too. "Watching you has been like a kick in the pants. I've been wallowing for the past year and here you are— you had your own disappointment and disillusionment, and you picked yourself up and went right on. Seeing it is letting me know that it's time for me to walk off my own disappointments and disillusionments. To stop letting them hold me back. To move on."

He was still running his index finger along the side of her face in a featherlight stroke that was soothing and arousing at once, sending something glittery all through her to make talking about Leo less depressing.

Then that finger reached the corner of her jawbone and slipped around it to come under her chin and tip it up.

And it wasn't only his life he was moving on with, because he moved on to kissing her...

At first Nina was taken off guard, and she thought again that he must not have hated the fact that she'd kissed him the night before.

Then all she could think about was the kiss that was happening at that moment.

A genuine kiss that lingered long enough for her to relish it.

And, oh, did she…

His lips were wonderful—soft and warm and lush. They were parted just slightly and his head swayed like a palm frond in a tropical breeze. The whole thing seemed to pick her up and carry her away to something so much nicer than what they'd been talking about, answering the yearning in her that she'd felt since he'd first kissed her during the blizzard. The yearning that had only been worse since the night before. The yearning that she didn't want to have but couldn't seem to stop no matter how hard she tried.

The yearning that wasn't at all stifled when that kiss came to an end a moment later.

She opened her eyes to Dallas's handsome face hovering just above hers, those same lips in one of his single-sided smiles, his gray-blue eyes studying her as if he liked what he saw.

"To moving on," he toasted in a deep, gravelly voice.

"To moving on," Nina seconded, feeling dazed and just wanting him to kiss her again.

But he didn't. He took a deep breath that

expanded his barrel chest and sighed with what sounded like resignation.

Then he said, "I'd better go. I have to be home when my folks bring the boys back."

Nina raised her chin higher in concession to that.

"But tomorrow night is the Candlelight Walk," he continued. "I'm gonna make sure that the boys experience every bit of Christmas festivity there is from now until the big day, so I told them we could go. I'd like it if you'd come with us—and I have a plan for getting you down Main Street since I wouldn't make you walk it."

All of Rust Creek Falls was invited to light a candle at one end of Main Street and parade with those candles to the opposite end where a bonfire was to be lit, carols were to be sung and refreshments would be served. It seemed as if the community had grown so much closer since the flood, and the city council had organized the walk as a method of bringing everyone together as the family of Rust Creek Falls before each separate family began their own private celebrations.

"You have a plan to get me down Main Street," Nina reiterated. "You don't think I can walk? You think I need a crane?"

He grinned, standing and making a show of helping her to her feet.

"It's a surprise," he said, rather than answering her accusation and affront.

"What if I say no?" she challenged as he put on his coat and they headed for her back door.

"Then you'll ruin the surprise."

There was that little bit of cockiness about him that was too delicious for her to resist.

"So don't say no," he added at the door with a challenge of his own.

Nina considered that his kiss and the continuing yearning for another one might be clouding her judgment.

But he had her intrigued.

And her own family had already decided to forego the walk because her parents and two of her brothers were helping out in the store all day tomorrow and wanted to just go home after closing, so she hadn't planned to go, either.

Only now she could.

With Dallas...

"Well, I wouldn't want to ruin a surprise," she finally conceded.

"Great! The candle lighting is at seven, so I'll be here about fifteen minutes before that."

"Crane and all?"

"Crane and all," he said, taking his turn at teasing her.

Then, with his hands in his coat pockets he leaned forward and kissed her again—a kiss as good as the earlier one had been—before he said, "Thanks for today."

Nina laughed. "*You* did me the favor by driving and helping out with the deliveries, then *you* made me dinner and cleaned the whole mess. Thank *you!*"

"I'm just glad I got to spend today and to-night with you. You're my inspiration, re-member?" he added.

"Ah, that's right. Because I'm so *inspirational,*" she joked.

His smoky-blue eyes delved deeply into hers. "More than you know," he seemed to confide.

Then he kissed her once more—barely, the way she'd kissed him the previous night—and went out into the cold.

And once Nina had closed the door behind him she stayed where she was, wrapping her arms around her pregnant belly, basking in the warm feelings that Dallas Traub had left her with.

Chapter 7

With only three days until Christmas, and Sunday the last weekend day before the holiday, Nina knew the store would be swamped. She and all of her staff and extra holiday personnel were scheduled, and she'd also asked her parents to come in.

Todd and Laura Crawford were semiretired, handling primarily behind-the-scenes business for the store now—ordering merchandise and doing the bookkeeping. But for Nina and the holiday they'd agreed to work the floor.

Nina expected them to arrive just before the store opened. She didn't expect them to arrive just as she was sitting down to breakfast.

"Have you eaten? I can scramble a few more eggs and make extra toast," she offered as they took off their coats.

"We ate," her mother answered, but both of her parents accepted glasses of orange juice as they sat at her small kitchen table and encouraged her to eat while her food was hot.

"We came early because we wanted to talk to you," her mother added as Nina put butter and jelly on her toast. "We've been hearing a lot about you and Dallas Traub."

"What's going on with that?" her father demanded.

"I've seen him a few times since the blizzard. He's helped out with the Santa's Workshop things—"

"From what we're hearing it sounds more like you're dating him," her mother accused, clearly not happy with the idea.

"I wouldn't say we were *dating.*" Nina balked at that term herself, despite the fact that the evening at the snow castle and the plan for the Candlelight Walk couldn't really be called anything else. "But we are—" she wasn't sure how to describe what they were and settled on "—friends, I guess."

"You're *friends* with a Traub?" her mother said as if even that was repugnant.

"I don't know why that's so awful to you," Nina responded, thinking that maybe she could reason with them. "After everything that Dallas did for me during the blizzard—"

"He ran you off the road." Her father again.

"I ran myself off the road. And him, too. And since then he's not only wanted to know how I'm doing, he's volunteered—"

"To get next to you," her mother insisted. "The Traubs are probably angling for something—"

"What could they possibly be *angling* for?"

"That's the problem," her father picked up where her mother had left off. "You don't *know* what they're angling for until they stab you in the back."

"Dallas is not positioning himself to stab me in the back," Nina asserted, unable to even imagine that.

"Maybe you don't know the Traubs like we do," her father suggested.

"Maybe you don't know them the way you think you do. I haven't heard anything that makes them sound any different than we are," Nina informed her parents firmly.

"No different than we are?" Her mother nearly shrieked as if that was inconceivable. "Have you forgotten the election?"

"I haven't forgotten that, like all politics, there was mudslinging from both sides," Nina reminded them pointedly.

"She's siding with the enemy," her father said to her mother.

Nina closed her eyes in frustration and shook her head. "*Why* are we enemies?" she demanded. "What do we really have to be enemies about? They run a ranch, we have a store—we're not business competitors. Yes, I'm sorry that Nate lost the election for mayor, but there have been other elections where a Crawford won and a Traub lost. And losing didn't ruin Nate's life. Nothing that I can think of about the Traubs has ruined any Crawford's life unless it was so long ago no one can even remember. So what's the big deal? They're regular people just like us—"

"Oh, my God, are you getting *involved* with Dallas Traub?" Laura Crawford said in horror.

Involved…

Did kissing count as that? Or wanting to kiss him again? Or finding herself beginning to crave more than kissing…?

No, she couldn't be getting *involved* with Dallas, Nina told herself. Becoming friends was one thing. Making any sort of headway in ending this ridiculous feud would be a good thing. But involved?

"No, I'm not getting *involved* with Dallas," she answered her mother's question in no uncertain terms because it needed not to be true.

He was too old for her. He might not think he was set in his ways but he had responsibilities that made it impossible for him *not* to be rooted in any number of obligations. A woman coming into his life would have to do plenty of adapting. Adapting that Nina wasn't willing to do yet again.

Especially not now, when she had her own baby to look forward to, to be responsible for, to become set in her own ways with without dragging that baby into a situation where it would have to adapt, too.

"But we also aren't enemies," Nina went on, deciding to be honest with her parents about that. "If you all want to go on hating a whole group of people just because somewhere a million years ago other Crawfords got into it with the Traubs, that's your business. But I can't for the life of me see why our families should be *feuding*. Just saying the word seems silly."

Todd looked at his wife and said, "She won't think it's silly when this Traub or another one does something spiteful or vengeful or just plain down-and-dirty to her."

"And one or another of them will," Laura agreed with her husband but aimed her comment at Nina. "And what worries me is that this time it's getting personal and you could get hurt. You and the baby…"

Nina sighed. "Dallas *saved* me and the baby. You think he would turn around and do something to hurt us now?"

"I think if you're having some kind of feelings for him it could very well happen, yes," Laura said direly. "Maybe that's his game— to suck you in with false charms and then kick you in the teeth and laugh about it."

Dallas was definitely charming. But there was nothing false about it. And as for the thought that he might be playing her, luring her in so he could do something to hurt her later? That was just ridiculous, and if her mother had been on the other side of those kisses the previous evening the way Nina had, Laura would know just how ludicrous it was.

"Why would he do something like that?" Nina asked, her tone reflecting the absurdity of it. "That doesn't even make sense. You think anyone would spend time *luring* one of us in just to be mean and then laugh about it later?"

"A Traub would," her father contended firmly and without the slightest doubt.

Nina could only roll her eyes. She had reasons enough not to get involved with Dallas, they just weren't the reasons her parents clung to. But since she *did* have reasons of her own, and since she could see that her parents weren't going to budge in their hatred of the Traubs—yet another reason why she knew she couldn't let things with Dallas go too far—she decided to stop arguing it.

"You don't have to worry," she told her parents as she took her breakfast dishes to the sink. "My path and Dallas's have crossed a few times, we are *not* enemies and I won't let you talk me into being enemies with him. But there isn't anything going on between us."

If kissing didn't count.

Except that it had counted.

A whole lot...

But she tried not to think about that. And vowed that it wouldn't happen again, telling herself that—for her reasons if not for her family's—she should probably start keeping some distance from him after tonight's Candlelight Walk.

Because she'd already agreed to that. And

she really wanted to go. And to see what kind of surprise he had for her.

But after that? Separate corners. She swore it.

For now, though, all Nina could do was announce that it was time they went down to the store and open up.

Thinking that no matter what it was that had the Crawfords and the Traubs hating each other, it seemed insurmountable.

As promised, Dallas arrived to pick up Nina for the Candlelight Walk just before seven that night. When she heard the knock on her back door she called for him to come in while she put on her final layer—a calf-length, double-breasted wool coat that she was wearing over her warmest knee-high boots, navy blue wool leggings, and a matching heavyweight turtleneck tunic.

As Dallas opened her unlocked door and stepped over the threshold she said, "Hi. Almost ready," and pulled a navy-blue-and-white tweed knit cap over her free-falling hair before putting on the matching scarf and gloves.

"Good—you're dressed nice and warm," he said, giving her the once-over and a smile that said he approved. And liked what he saw.

"You look warm, too." And she liked what she saw just as much—he was wearing boots, jeans and a brown henley sweater over a tan turtleneck T-shirt that were all barely visible underneath his shearling-lined suede coat.

"My truck is parked in front of the store but I had some help bringing your surprise, and that's out back," he said with a grin.

"Then let's go," Nina said.

Her surprise was waiting for them at the foot of her back steps—a horse-drawn sleigh.

"She's a two-seater bobsleigh," Dallas informed her as he followed Nina down the stairs. "The swan body shape makes her an Albany."

Polished bronze sides and a swooping back surrounded two fairly narrow rows of tufted black velvet seats, front and back. The three Traub boys were sitting close together in the rear to fit, and Robbie was bouncing up and down in his excitement.

"Lookit this," he commanded Nina. "I din't even know we had it! It's like Santa's sleigh!"

"It's beautiful, isn't it?" she answered the smallest boy's enthusiasm with some of her own, taking in the sight of the red ribbon–wrapped pine boughs attached to the gracefully curved top edge, and more red ribbons braided into the reins.

"That's Toad and Trina pullin' us." Robbie introduced the horses, whose harnesses bore bells and more red ribbons.

"Hi, Ryder. Hi, Jake. Hi, Toad and Trina," Nina greeted them.

"Hi," the other boys responded in unison, both of them sitting up straight enough to make it clear they were excited, too. Particularly Ryder, who held the reins as if he'd been given a very important responsibility.

"Come on, let's go!" Jake urged.

"Okay, okay, hold your horses," Dallas said, making an obvious joke as he offered a leather-gloved hand for Nina to take so he could help her into the sleigh.

"We'll have the candlelight ride rather than the candlelight walk?" Nina took that hand, and regretted his glove and hers keeping her from too much sensation.

"We will," he confirmed as she sat on the plush seat.

Dallas went around the rear to get into the other side. Because the sleigh wasn't wide they were arm to arm, and Nina had to resist the urge to snuggle in even closer.

Then Dallas turned to get the reins from Ryder and Nina said, "There's no snowpack left on Main Street—is this going to work?"

"I won't say it's good for the runners but I waxed them pretty heavily and we won't be going far, so it should be okay."

A tap of the reins on the horses' backs and the animals took them from behind Crawford's General Store onto Sawmill Street and around to Main.

The store was at the high end of Main—which was what had spared it from the flood damage—and most of the town was gathering there, lighting candles and getting ready to start the walk.

Dallas pulled up behind the crowd and sent Ryder for two of the candles that were being given out by the city council. When Ryder returned with them, Dallas lit them and set them in holders nestled amid the ribbon-wrapped boughs on the front corners of the sleigh.

"Isn't that pretty?" Nina asked, angling her comment and her own enthusiasm toward the boys in back and making sure they could see.

Minutes later the walk began, and again Dallas urged the horses to move, setting them to a very slow pace. Up ahead the parade of people, all carrying candles, lit the way with the tiny flickers of so many flames casting a beautiful golden glow.

"Oh, this is so nice," Nina breathed, putting her family's feelings about the Traubs to rest for the time being so she could just enjoy the festivities.

The procession down Main Street didn't take long, and when the first of the walkers reached the park where the bonfire was laid in a contained area, Nina craned to watch and said to the boys, "Stand up so you can see—they're lighting the bonfire!"

The sleigh was moving so slowly there was no danger to the boys in standing for the remainder of the ride that took them alongside the park where those of the community who hadn't been inclined to walk down Main Street had parked in advance.

One big *whoosh* and the entire area was alight with flames, causing the crowd to gasp before they cheered and clapped.

After that, an announcement was made that there were marshmallows to be toasted, as well as one table where hot chocolate or cider could be had and another that held Christmas goodies of all kinds.

Then the church choir began to sing carols and the crowd started to mingle.

While Nina was the only one of the Crawfords to come, the Traubs had made a good showing. Dallas's parents and brothers Collin, Braden and Sutter were all there. Tense but polite greetings were exchanged with Nina before Dallas allowed the boys to have their way and drag them to roast marshmallows, cutting the encounter blissfully short.

Collin's wife, Willa, and Sutter's fiancée, Paige Dalton, were also with that group and had greeted Nina more warmly. Then, on their way to the beverage table, they made a second stop with Dallas and Nina and the boys. Paige was Ryder's fifth-grade teacher, Willa had Robbie in kindergarten, and they both wanted to wish all three boys a personal Merry Christmas.

As Nina, Dallas and the boys roasted marshmallows in one of many little fires that were lit in small flame-safe boxes around the bonfire, Nina and Dallas exchanged hellos and small talk with local veterinarian Brooks Smith and his new wife, Jazzy.

"Oh, look," Jazzy said after a few minutes of that, "Dean Pritchett and Shelby are here!"

She waved the couple over. Dean Pritchett was a carpenter who had come from Thunder Canyon to help with some of the rebuilding after the flood and fallen in love with substitute teacher and single mom Shelby Jenkins.

They joined the group, along with Shelby's daughter, Caitlin, whom Nina shared her marshmallows with.

"And Sheriff!" Dallas said as Gage Christensen and his fiancée, Lissa Roarke, walked up to them, hand in hand.

Gage told Nina he was glad to see that she was doing all right after the blizzard scare, and Nina thanked him again for his help that day.

During Lissa's volunteer work in Rust Creek Falls, she and the sheriff had become involved—and eventually engaged—and now that they were part of the small group, talk just naturally turned to the ongoing flood projects. At least, it did until Shane Roarke brought his marshmallow to their little roasting station.

Shane Roarke was Dallas's cousin and had only recently learned that his father was Thunder Canyon's notorious ex-mayor Arthur Swinton. The notorious Swinton was currently in prison for embezzling funds from Thunder Canyon.

It was common knowledge that Shane and his adopted siblings, Los Angeles attorneys Maggie and Ryan Roarke, were attempting to get Arthur's prison sentence commuted, so conversation turned to questions about how things were going with that.

Nina only heard, "We're making headway," as the answer to those questions before the three Traub boys, tired of listening to adult conversation, urged Dallas and Nina to take them to the cookie table.

Telling everyone they had to go and exchanging more wishes for a Merry Christmas, Nina and Dallas moved on to the table that held not only cookies but brownies, cakes, cupcakes and fudge.

Each boy was allotted only one choice—and complained about it—before Collin came to tell Dallas that the family had had enough of the cold and was leaving.

"Can we go with 'em? I'm cold, too," Robbie piped up when he heard that.

"Me, too," Jake chimed in.

"Yeah, my feet are freezing," Ryder added.

"Mom!" Dallas called across the distance that his parents were keeping from them. "Can you take the boys home for me? I'll pick them up in a while."

"Sure. Come on," she urged her grandsons. "I want to get going."

Dallas prompted his sons to say goodnight to Nina, and then Nina and Dallas both watched as Collin herded them off with the rest of the Traubs.

"It *is* cold," Nina said.

It was the truth. But it was also the truth that she'd had a very long, hard day and was longing to just sit in front of her own fireplace.

"You know, we *could* go back and light a fire at my place, and I could mull us a little cider…"

"You're cold, too," Dallas guessed.

"A little bit."

"Yeah, I'm feeling it myself," he confessed. "So you don't have to ask me twice. Just give me a minute…"

He left Nina standing there while he went to talk to a teenage boy Nina didn't recognize, and then he and the teenager came back.

"Okay, let's go," Dallas said, only mentioning after the fact, on the way to the sleigh, that the teenager who was following them was Tyson, the son of one of his ranch hands.

"Tyson brought the sleigh out for me and he's going to take us to your place in it, then get it home for me." Leaning close to Nina's ear he whispered, "I'm paying him well for his services."

For the trip back to her apartment, Dallas and Nina sat in the rear row while Tyson took the front and the reins.

There was a blanket that the boys had apparently been sitting on, and Dallas opened it over their laps. When he tucked it in around them Nina had a flashback to the blizzard and being alone with him in his truck.

Although it seemed strange that an experience such as a near collision and fearing she was going into premature labor in the middle of nowhere could become a fond memory, it somehow had. And she read that as another sign that things between them might be stretching the boundaries.

But then he settled back with her shoulder cozily against his and told the teenager they were ready, and all Nina could think about was how much she liked being there like that with him.

The return trip to her apartment was much quicker than the procession to the bonfire had been. Then Dallas helped her out of the sleigh, dispatching Tyson to get it home.

Nina led the way up her back steps and into her apartment, the heat there feeling blissful after being out in the cold for so long.

"How are *you* at building a fire?" Nina asked as they took off their outerwear.

"Fires in fireplaces, campfires, bonfires, burning off weeds—seems like I've been building them all my life. Want me to do this one?" he asked, pointing his chin in the direction of her hearth.

"If you would. Kindling and logs are in the bucket right beside it. I'll do the cider and meet you there."

"Sounds like a deal."

Nina left him to it. But because this portion of her apartment was basically one big room, she could steal glimpses of him while she heated and spiced the cider. Hunkered down in front of her fireplace, his thick thighs stretching the denim of his jeans, and his very, very fine derriere resting on the heels of his boots, he was a sexy sight that she cautioned herself against appreciating as much as she was.

But she still couldn't help it. He was just all man—big and brawny and muscular and masculine—and she thought she would have had to be dead not to recognize that fact.

And she definitely wasn't dead. In fact, she knew she was awash in extra hormones that made it especially difficult for the woman in her not to be extraordinarily aware of him.

Still, she tried to tamp down on it as she brought two mugs of steaming cider into the living room, where he had, indeed, built a beautiful fire.

"Oh, that feels good," Nina said as she joined him. "Why don't we move the coffee table and sit on the floor in front of the couch so we can be closer to the fire?"

Agreeing, Dallas held both cups while she eased herself down, tucking her feet to one side and watching as he sat beside her and tasted his cider.

"Mmm, that's perfect," he judged.

Nina took a sip of hers, too, then said, "So, Arthur Swinton…" referring to the man who had become the subject of conversation just before they'd left the marshmallow-toasting station earlier. "I've never been too clear about him. Seems like he was a big shot in Thunder Canyon, then a bad guy who went to jail, then I thought I heard he was dead, then he wasn't, and now people seem to be saying positive things about him again."

"Yeah, that all sounds about right," Dallas answered. "You know we just learned that Shane Roarke—who is Arthur Swinton's biological son—is actually our cousin?"

"I think I did hear something about that," Nina said vaguely.

"Yeah, Shane was raised by adoptive parents, with a brother and a sister who were also adopted. Then he found out that Arthur Swinton was his biological father and that Grace Traub—one of our Thunder Canyon relations—was his biological mother. Grace died a long time ago, but apparently, when she was in her late teens, she was involved with Swinton and got pregnant, then gave the baby up."

"There are Traubs in Thunder Canyon, and here—you guys are all over the place."

"In Texas, too," he said. "But Thunder Canyon was where Swinton was."

Somewhat larger than Rust Creek Falls—and only three hundred or so miles south—Thunder Canyon had prospered in recent years, and because there were many connections between the two towns a number of its residents had gone to great lengths to assist their neighbors in Rust Creek Falls since the flood.

"He was on Thunder Canyon's town council for years and he even ran for mayor a while back. Then somebody figured out that he'd been embezzling funds from Thunder Canyon—"

"Oh, that's right—*that's* why he was in jail," Nina said.

"Swinton wouldn't say what happened to the money or where it was hidden—if it was hidden—"

"And it was rumored that he'd died in jail…"

"Uh-huh. Except that he really just escaped. Then he was recaptured—"

"So, not dead," Nina said, making Dallas laugh.

"No, not dead. And at that point he was pretty widely considered Thunder Canyon's villain. Then folks found out about him having a son—"

"Shane Roarke."

"Right. Shane. But Grace never told Swinton she was pregnant. She went out of town to have Shane and put him up for adoption. When Shane found out Swinton was his father he came from California to Thunder Canyon and let Swinton know. When word got around, public opinion softened for Swinton. There's been some sympathy for him not getting to see his son grow up. Now Shane and his adopted siblings, Ryan and Maggie— who are both attorneys—are working on getting him out of jail."

"I heard some talk about Arthur Swinton raising money for Rust Creek Falls."

"Yeah, Shane claims that he's somehow managed to do that, even from prison. We haven't seen the money yet, but Shane believes that it's a legitimate campaign and that something is going to come of it. As a symbol of Swinton's goodwill."

"I hope for your cousin's sake that that's true. And for Rust Creek Falls' sake, too—we could certainly use the money to help with the reconstruction."

"But the school is about finished. I heard today that it'll be reopening after winter break, which is great. It's getting to be a pain to take all three kids to three different places for their classes."

"I'm sure!" Nina commiserated.

For a moment they sat quietly, enjoying the fire and the cider until their cups were empty and set aside on the floor.

Then Dallas said, "Speaking of school, tomorrow night is the Christmas program. It's always kind of a hoot and makes me feel like Christmas is really here. They're having to do it in the social hall at the church this year, but the boys and I wondered if you might like to see it? It'll give you a preview of Christmases to come," he said with a nod in the direction of her middle.

"I'd love that!" Nina heard herself answer before she'd considered what she was agreeing to, acting solely on impulse. Then she remembered that she'd told herself to start keeping her distance from Dallas and realized this wouldn't aid *that* cause.

"But won't your family be there?" she asked, seizing one of the multiple reasons she'd told herself to keep that distance in the first place.

"Yep," he confirmed with a note of defiance underlying his tone. "But the boys asked me to invite you, so everyone else will just have to deal with it."

The boys had asked her. It wasn't Dallas's idea.

No sooner had that thought crossed Nina's mind than Dallas seemed to read it. He turned to face her, peering into her eyes. Using his index and middle fingers he brushed her hair over her shoulder and confided in a quieter voice, "And how could I deny them when it's what I want, too?"

Looking into that handsome face of his, those gray-blue eyes staring into hers—it was a lethal combination that sank all of Nina's better judgment.

All of it.

Because when he kissed her, she was right there with him, kissing him back. And unable to think about anything except that kiss and that it was what she'd been wanting since the minute he'd stopped kissing her the night before.

And, oh, what a kiss…

Saturday's kiss had been good, but this one was even better. Deeper right from the start.

His mouth was pressed more insistently to hers. His lips were parted farther and more sensuously, and she only realized after the fact that hers were, too.

And then there was his tongue…talented, enticing, tempting hers into a coy fencing match, upping the level of intimacy.

And Nina gave as good as she got, still thinking about nothing but that kiss and him, and how much she just wanted to go on and on kissing him.

Which was what she did. What they did. For a long while. Making out there in front of the fire, things heating up between them that the fire had nothing to do with.

His arms had come around her, her hands were in his hair and he was holding her tightly against him. So tightly that her breasts, fuller these days, were smooshed to his unyielding chest, blissfully pressing into him, her nipples turning to insistent little peaks that she wondered if he could feel. That were beginning to cause her to think about more than the mere pressure of even his rock-solid pectorals.

Oh, yeah, kissing this way was only making her want more!

So much more that it gave Nina pause.

She wasn't even supposed to kiss him again. Let alone for the entire past half hour. And the way they'd been kissing.

Distance, she reminded herself. Separate corners…

Less, not more…

Whether she liked it or not… She drew her hands down, her shoulders back and pushed on Dallas's shoulders. Pushed him away.

And he got the idea.

Reluctantly tongues retreated, leaving mouths to linger for another moment before they parted, too. Before the kissing that Nina wanted never to end, ended anyway.

Dallas took a deep breath and raised his head high enough to tuck hers under his chin, staying that way as he exhaled.

Then he said a musing, "Huh…how'd that happen?" As if he wasn't quite sure what had just carried them away.

"The cider was not hard or spiked," Nina joked in a soft voice, her face burrowed into his neck.

"Let's blame—"

"The spices?" Nina suggested.

"Or just the damn smell of your hair that goes right to my head…"

"The shampoo, then." Nina went on joking because she knew at that point that she had to lighten the mood. Or give in to it…

And she couldn't give in to it.

"Yeah, the shampoo," he agreed reluctantly, taking another deep breath and sitting back as he took her by the shoulders and repositioned her several inches away from him.

Then he said, "I believe we were talking about an innocent elementary school Christmas program…"

"We were," she confirmed, knowing without a doubt now that she shouldn't go.

"The program starts at seven, the boys have to be there at six, so what if I take them to the church, get them situated, then sneak over here and pick you up?"

Say no…

But out loud she said, "I'll be ready."

Dallas smiled as if he'd known she'd been thinking about turning him down after all and he was relieved that she hadn't.

Then he got to his feet, held out both hands to help her to her feet, as well, and they went to her door. He took his coat from where he'd hung it on the doorknob and put it on.

He looked at her the entire time, studying her, and then he shook his head and said more to himself than to her, "Nina *Crawford...*"

And this time she knew what he was thinking—that of all the people for whatever was happening to be happening, it was happening between a Crawford and a Traub.

Then he breathed deeply, sighed it out as if in some kind of concession and leaned forward to kiss her again—a long, sweet, sexy kiss that could well have started everything all over again had he not pulled away quickly.

Another deep breath, a sigh, a last lingering look into her eyes, and he opened the door and left.

And Nina wilted against it once it was shut.

Knowing that distance and separate corners were not at all what she wanted, in spite of what she'd sworn to herself earlier.

What she really wanted was Dallas.

Any way.

Any time.

Anywhere.

Chapter 8

The school Christmas program on Monday evening was funny and endearing and full of foibles. There were heartfelt, off-key Christmas songs—one per grade that advanced from the timid singing of the kindergarteners—who forgot some of the words—to the far more polished sixth graders. There were skits. There was a sixth-grade girl band with an overly loud drummer doing a rendition of "Rockin' Around the Christmas Tree." And the diamond in the crown was the production of "'Twas the Night Before Christmas."

The students enacted the poem while one of the older girls read it. A kindergartner in a mouse costume pretended to sleep, but couldn't keep her eyes closed.

A fourth grader played Santa in a costume stuffed with a pillow that was sticking out from under his cottonball-edged red jacket. He was also wearing a beard that was askew in one direction while his hat was off-kilter in the other, and his boots were black galoshes.

The sleigh was a red wagon with cardboard sides resembling Dallas's bobsleigh— not surprisingly, since Ryder had worked on the scenery and staging. But one of the sides fell off midplay.

The reindeer wore brown construction-paper antlers, with Jake in the lead wearing a red clown nose.

Some license was taken. The father was at the cardboard cutout window, but so was Mama in her kerchief as well as the two children who rose from their visions of sugar-plums to witness Santa's ride.

Robbie was the youngest child of the pajama-clad family, although rather than watching Santa, Robbie scanned the audience for his father and waved when he spotted Dallas and Nina.

In the process of that, Robbie didn't see it coming when the nightgown-clad mother of the group tripped on her hem and fell into him, causing them to tumble and barely avoid falling off the stage.

Robbie's loud "Jeez, Janey," was answered by Janey's "It's this dumb nightgown," interrupting the performance and making the audience laugh.

By the time Mama in her kerchief got back to her feet and Robbie did, too, the narrator had lost her place and reread a few lines before getting to the only other dialogue in the play—Santa calling "Happy Christmas to all, and to all a good-night!"

Clapping and cheers and whistles rewarded the performance along with a standing ovation as everyone who had participated in the rest of the program, too, returned to the stage to take their final bows.

Robbie was at the very front, and he dramatically hid one arm behind his back, crossed the other over his stomach and took a very deep bow as if the accolades were all for him.

Then the announcement came that refreshments were being set out at the back of the social hall, the kids got down from the stage to find their families and the mingling began—the portion of the evening that Nina had been dreading.

Dallas's parents had arrived before Dallas and Nina, and Dallas had urged Nina into the two free seats directly in front of them. Restrained hellos had been exchanged with Nina from there, just moments before the lights were dimmed so no more had had to be said.

But now Nina knew there was bound to be more of an encounter and she wasn't sure what would happen. Although she had been with Dallas and the boys at the bonfire, and the Traubs had been sort of civil, it hadn't seemed quite as couple-ish as sitting beside him through the program, and she wasn't sure how that would be viewed.

Especially when she had no doubt that every time Dallas had leaned over to whisper some comment into her ear, every time they'd cast each other a smile, the older Traubs had been watching.

She was right that there was no avoiding Dallas's parents. By the time all three boys found them, the four adults had met at the end of the row of seats to stand together.

At first the focus of the adults was on the boys, complimenting them for their parts in the various portions of the program. But then the boys wanted refreshments and their grandfather volunteered to take them, leaving Nina and Dallas alone with Ellie Traub.

Who was staring pointedly at her son.

But just when Nina was afraid the other woman was going to say something negative, she instead said to Dallas, "It's nice to see you like this."

"Mom. I saw you three times today at home and we're together at all these school things—are you losing it or what?" Dallas said, clearly perplexed by the comment that made it sound as if this encounter was out of the ordinary.

"It's nice to see you not down in the dumps," his mother amended, glancing at Nina.

Nina barely knew the woman. When any Traub did come into the store they were always curt and civil, and they got out again as quickly as they could.

But tonight something was different. And Nina thought what she was seeing in Ellie Traub's expression was acceptance. Reluctant acceptance, but acceptance just the same.

Then, in a more friendly, conversational tone, Ellie Traub said, "How do you spend the holidays, Nina? With your family, I expect."

"Usually. At my parents' house," Nina answered. "Christmas Eve *and* Christmas Day. But between yesterday and today, everyone except my mom and me came down with the flu, so my mom is playing nurse. She called just before I left tonight to tell me I've been banned from getting anywhere near them."

"So, no Christmas?" Dallas asked, alarmed.

Nina shrugged. "Mom said we'll just have a belated one when this passes—we'll exchange our gifts, have the same foods we planned, do it all the way we always do, but in a week or so."

"We have a big dinner Christmas Eve—friends and family—why don't you come?" Ellie Traub invited her instantly.

Nina wasn't the only one shocked by that. She saw Dallas's eyebrows arch, and for a moment he looked as if he wasn't sure he'd heard correctly.

But his mother ignored both of their reactions and went on as if she hadn't just extended a major olive branch to the enemy. "We have tons of food—I always cook for an army, don't I, Dallas? And this year we're doing even more, making it even bigger. I saw the way the boys were with you—I'm sure they'd like it if you'd come." She cast a glance at her son, making Nina think that Ellie Traub was including Dallas as one of the *boys*.

"We'd *all* like it if you'd come," the older woman added.

It was on the tip of Nina's tongue to say: you *would?* And she couldn't quite think of anything else to say.

Then Dallas chimed in. "Come. We can't have you spending it alone."

"Oh, it's all right. No big deal. I'll be fine..."

"I insist, Nina! It's against our house policy to let anyone be alone at Christmas," Ellie Traub informed her. "Dallas will pick you up at six. Won't you, Dallas?"

The older woman looked at her son and smiled a loving, knowing smile.

"I will," he confirmed.

Then Bob Traub brought the boys back, delivering cookies to his wife and son while Robbie handed a frosting-decorated wreath to Nina.

"I called it first so I got to bring yours," he announced, as if it were a coup.

Nina thanked him, and after they'd all eaten their cookies Ellie Traub suggested that she and Bob take the boys home and get them to bed while Dallas took Nina. That seemed like the second seal of approval for them to be together.

Which they weren't, Nina reminded herself. They weren't *together.* But if his mother was conceding that they might be friends, that was okay. So that was how she chose to view it.

Then the boys followed Dallas's instructions to put on their coats, to mind their grandparents and go right to bed when they got home, and goodbyes were said.

"We'll see you tomorrow night," Ellie Traub told Nina as she left, drawing a surprised glance from Bob.

Then, in the process of urging their grandsons to the door, Nina heard Ellie Traub answer that surprise. "He's better, Bob, and I'm glad for whatever or whoever did it."

"Sooo... I'm thinking that a perk of hanging out with the owner is that maybe I could do a little last-minute Christmas shopping even though the store is closed..." Dallas suggested hopefully, as he opened his truck's passenger door for Nina to get out.

Conversation on the drive from the church to Nina's apartment had been about the funny points of the Christmas program, so this was a change of subject.

"Oh, really..." Nina responded.

"Not that the biggest perk isn't just getting to hang out with you," he claimed. "But tomorrow is Christmas Eve and I have a million things to do, and I still need a few stocking stuffers for the boys. I was just thinking that here we are—"

"Right above all those things in the store," Nina finished for him as she unlocked the outside door to her apartment and went in, turning on lights as she did.

"Unless going down there after hours will trigger an alarm system or security cameras will record it and alert the sheriff to come running or something..."

"I can bypass the security system, and we don't have cameras. Maybe next year, but not yet," Nina told him as they took off their coats.

Tonight she was wearing a longish wrap-around gray sweater over slim-leg jeans with knee-high black boots whose three-inch heels she knew her obstetrician wouldn't have approved of. But, pregnant or not, she had no intention of looking dowdy—a fact that seemed to be more and more of an issue whenever she was dressing to see Dallas.

Dallas, who looked fabulous in a heavy-weight tan field sweater and jeans that showed off a great rear end.

Something she knew she shouldn't have noticed.

"So, if we can bypass the security system

and there aren't any cameras to record my special treatment…" he said, as if he were proposing being cat burglars, wiggling his eyebrows provocatively at the same time. "What do you say?"

"I suppose that, since I really liked getting a taste of what it will be like to be a parent at my kid's school Christmas program, I can reciprocate with a little extra store access." Nina conceded what she would have agreed to, in any event, just because it was Dallas asking.

"Then fire up a cash register and let's do it!" he said enthusiastically, making Nina laugh at him.

The panel that controlled the alarm system was on the second floor at the top of the steps that led down to the store. She punched in the code and then turned on half of the store lights. "We don't want to make it look like I'm open for business or, believe me, we'll have people knocking on the door and wanting to come in," she explained.

"Okay, then. You keep a lookout while I shop and I'll keep a lookout while you ring me up. Anyone comes to the door or the windows and we both go down," he said, again in cat-burglar mode.

"Deal," Nina agreed as they went into the dimly lit store.

While Dallas browsed, Nina lurked behind a partition, peeking out periodically to watch the front of the store and at the same time taking cans of pumpkin from a box to stack for the next day.

"Have you had any word from Laurel?" Nina asked, while Dallas picked out three yoyos and moved on to other small games intended to be stocking stuffers.

"My ex? No, not a peep," Dallas answered.

"Not a card or a letter? No gifts for the boys?"

"Nothing."

"I guess something could still come tomorrow. Mail will be delivered and so will packages," Nina said, hoping that the mother of Dallas's children wouldn't let this oh-so-important holiday go by without acknowledging those kids.

"I think, since each of their birthdays came and went this year without anything from her, they know better than to expect something now."

"Oh, that's right..." Nina said, recalling that he'd told her Laurel had let each of the boys' birthdays pass unacknowledged. Even so, it didn't seem any less awful for Ryder, Jake and Robbie's mother not to send them Christmas gifts.

"Still," she said, "they're little kids. There's got to be some tiny bit of hope, deep down, that she'll do something. And then when— if—she doesn't, it will put a damper on things for them."

"You're probably right," Dallas said, somewhat grimly, picking out three stocking-stuffer-size footballs. "I guess I like to think they've forgotten about her, that they don't care, and since they haven't said anything it makes it easier on me, but—"

"You know they *do* care."

"Yeah…" Dallas said reflectively. "Sure they do. Robbie trying to get her his school picture shows they haven't forgotten her—no matter how I'd like to delude myself."

"Have you thought of wrapping something up for them and putting her name on it so they *think* she sent them something?"

Dallas stopped sorting through tiny puzzle boxes to look at her. "Huh…" he mused. "No, that didn't occur to me. Do you think I should?"

Nina hadn't actually put any thought into it before she'd said it, but now she did. "I don't know…" she said. "I can't imagine that you want to do anything that makes her look good when she's done such awful things and hasn't bothered with those kids herself. But would it be good for them to believe she thought about them?"

"Or would it be raising false hopes?"

"Do you think they *don't* hope every day that she'll come back?" Nina asked, verbally tiptoeing.

Dallas had chosen three puzzles, but he paused before putting them into the basket he was carrying, clearly considering that question, too. "I suppose they might," he conceded. "I did for a while, at first. Even with the cheating and how tough things had been…there was probably about a month where I even thought I saw her just about everywhere I looked, as if she might show up around the next corner. I never talked about it, but, yeah, the boys probably did the same thing. Except where I came to grips with the fact that she wasn't coming back, it makes sense that they might just wish she *would* show up again."

That was such a sad thought. And Nina could tell by the frown etched into Dallas's square brow that he thought so, too.

Then he said, "I don't know if Ryder would actually believe it. Or even Jake."

"But they'd try because they'd want to…" Nina said in a voice barely above a whisper, wondering if she was pressuring him. Hoping not. "You could write on the tags that she still won't be coming back, but that she just wanted them to have something—maybe that would help keep their hopes from being raised. But at least they'd feel remembered—"

"Even if they aren't," Dallas muttered.

Nina thought she'd said enough. And since Dallas seemed to be thinking about the whole issue, she left him to that.

Then he said, "I'm not putting her name on anything so great they'll like it better than what I bought them."

Nina suppressed a smile at that hint of stubbornness. "You could get them shirts. Shirts are kind of a mom thing. But not exciting to little boys."

Dallas didn't say anything, but Nina saw him move from the part of the store where the stocking stuffers were displayed to a table of boys' wear.

"There's not a part of me that wants to make her look good," he confessed, even as he picked out three shirts in varying sizes and colors. "But she's their damn mother, and it's Christmas, and I don't want them feeling any worse than they probably already do because it was this time last year when she left. If the chance to believe their mother remembered them helps any…well, I guess it's worth it."

Nina joined him to take three boxes from the shelf below the display. "Let me wrap them in some of the paper we have here so they won't be wrapped in what their other presents are in—it would be a dead giveaway."

Dallas nodded. "Thanks," he said.

Nina knew what he was doing wasn't easy for him. That it wasn't something he could do wholeheartedly, but that for the sake of his sons he was burying his own resentments, and she admired that. *Him.* So much that she couldn't keep herself from reaching a hand to his arm for a squeeze of support for his selflessness. "I don't know if this is the right thing to do or not, but you're a good dad for doing it."

"It was you who came up with it," he said. "And thanks for that, too," he added with a genuine smile. "Thanks for thinking of my boys. Of what might help them get through this."

Nina almost said they just made a good team but stopped short, reminding herself that she and Dallas *weren't* a team. That they couldn't be. Even though she liked the feel of his arm in her hand so much she never wanted to let go...

"I'll scan these and wrap them while you finish shopping," she said instead, forcing herself to take her hand away from his bulging biceps.

"Thanks for everything you've done," he added. "I'm not sure I would have gotten through this holiday without you..."

"You'd have done fine," Nina demurred.

Still keeping an eye on the front windows and door, she stayed as much out of sight as she could, and by the time she had three nicely wrapped shirt boxes, Dallas was finished with his shopping and ready for her to check him out.

Or, at least, to check out the items he was purchasing. She was trying *not* to check *him* out, despite the fact that her gaze kept drifting to him and getting stuck on him. Taking in every tiny detail. Liking it all...

The guy was just terrific-looking and it seemed impossible for her *not* to notice.

Terrific-looking and sooo sexy...

And that muscular arm she'd felt in his sweater sleeve had been big and rock-solid and—

And she'd decided this morning that it certainly must be pregnancy hormones that were putting her into overdrive when it came to Dallas, and that she wasn't going to be at the mercy of something like that.

So checking out his items was the only checking out she was going to do!

When she'd accomplished her task Dallas took his bag and they headed for the steps. But just as they reached them they heard voices from outside the front door.

"Are they open?" one voice asked.

"Some of the lights are on..."

Dallas dropped his bag, grabbed Nina and spun her around behind the wall that partitioned off a corridor to the employees' break room.

"Do you think they saw us?" Nina asked from where Dallas had her pinned to the wall.

"I don't know. They're trying the door. I didn't recognize them, though, did you?"

"No. Probably out-of-towners visiting somebody for the holidays."

"Let's just lay low for a few minutes," Dallas suggested. "Eventually they'll give up."

Nina laughed. "Or I could just holler out that we're closed..."

"And risk a story that will make us feel bad if we don't open up?" he asked, as if it were life or death. "Besides," he added with that lopsided smile of his, "this is so much more fun."

There was insinuation in his voice, making it clear that their position was the fun part. And certainly Nina couldn't find any fault in being backed up against a wall by him, the clean woodsy scent of his cologne going to her head and his superbly handsome face just inches above her...

"And since you're shielding me with your body I'm protected from grenade attacks, too," she joked in a feeble attempt to hint that he should move, at least trying to alter things.

But Dallas merely countered with, "Can't be too careful." And he didn't move. Instead he peered down into her eyes, grinning, making it clear that he liked it right where they were.

"You're so beautiful..." he whispered.

"Sure I am," she answered, making light of it. "Eight-and-a-half-months pregnant, and I've never looked better."

"I don't know about that, but I do know that little basketball belly you're sporting doesn't take anything away from those big brown eyes, or that peaches-and-cream skin, or that hair that's like...that's like heaven..."

He brushed the tip of her nose with the tip of his. "And I also know that it doesn't take away from the fact that when I'm with you I feel like a new man."

He looked into her eyes again with pure warmth in his. And a glint that told her what was coming.

His arms were already around her, his head was already tilted in her direction and their mouths were mere inches apart. And when he closed those inches to kiss her, Nina just naturally tipped her chin up and met him halfway.

Somehow, it had come to seem as if being with him wasn't complete until he kissed her, and once he started, she couldn't make herself stop it. She just loved kissing him so much....

Mouths and tongues knew the dance well by then, and there was no hesitation, no inhibition, just really, really good kissing, and kissing and more kissing.

Nina's eyes were closed and it didn't matter to her where they were. It only mattered that Dallas was holding her, that her own hands were fanned out across his wide shoulders, that they dropped down to the biceps she wanted another feel of, massaging and gripping muscles that barely gave way beneath her strongest grasp.

The kissing grew more fevered, and breaths came deeper, heavier, thrusting Nina's breasts into contact with Dallas's chest.

Her nipples were taut little diamonds. And so, so sensitive. More now than they'd ever been before. More, at that moment, than she could ever have believed possible, so that just that much contact brought them alive.

She didn't know if it was the extra fullness that her breasts had now, too, but they felt as if they were ready to burst from her bra. The bra that—the same way she wouldn't concede to flat shoes—hadn't yet been replaced with maternity bras. A bigger size, yes. But still lacy and lovely, and suddenly feeling much too confining.

Dallas's hands were on her back, rubbing and massaging divinely, and doing there what she was doing to his arms. What she suddenly wanted desperately to feel on her breasts.

She sent her hands to travel to his neck, to his nape, then up to comb her fingers through his hair as kissing became even more sensual, as tongues chased each other, and darted and thrust with intent.

Nina pressed her front more firmly to his—and then she felt Dallas insinuate a hand under the back of her sweater…

It took everything she had not to cry out, *yes! Yes! Yes!*

But all she did was give a more sensual twist of her tongue, and ease back the tiniest bit to provide enough room for his hand, even as deep breaths brought her chest to his like ocean waves to the shore, receding and returning lest he forget…

His other hand, massive and strong, callused, joined the first under her sweater, on her bare back. A rancher's hands, they coursed upward, working her shoulders for a few minutes before one of them drifted down. To the outer side of her breast.

She moaned her encouragement, almost dying inside for want of having him just get there.

And then he finally did—he drew his hand around to take her breast in it.

A quiet purr of pleasure rumbled in her throat, but it wasn't complete. Because that stupid, stupid bra was there! Keeping her from having what she really wanted.

And she just couldn't stand it. Not a single minute longer.

Almost on their own, her hands dropped from the back of Dallas's head, reached behind her and unhooked the bra…

A split second later she could hardly believe what she'd done.

But suddenly Dallas was kissing her in a way she'd never been kissed before, plundering her mouth with more sexual fervor than she thought a kiss could have. And both of his hands were on both of her breasts. His bare hands on her bare breasts. And that was all that mattered.

Never had she known anything to feel as fabulously intense. Every sensation, every tiny nuance was heightened. Every stroke, every knead, every tug, every caress, every squeeze. Every gentle pinch and roll of her nipples between his fingertips. Every feather-stroke brush against the very crest. Every supreme touch.

And the moan that answered it all came from depths she didn't even know she had.

As one hand shared time with each breast, his other hand returned to her back, splaying there to brace her for the full impact of what he was doing to breasts that couldn't get enough of him, and Nina began to wonder what it would be like to have his mouth on them instead...

Then Dallas pulled her in tighter, as if he just couldn't get enough of her. And that basketball-size belly he'd mentioned earlier came up against him…

Nothing about that gave him even the slightest pause.

But it was different for Nina.

It reminded her that she wasn't in a shape she'd ever been in before. And while she'd reveled in each change her baby had brought to her body, a jolt of self-consciousness hit her then, stopping her a little short.

Dallas sensed it instantly, and everything did pause then.

His hands stopped all movement. He ended their kissing. And concern was in his voice when he whispered, "Are you okay?"

This time her moan was bereft.

"I'm okay, but… I just… I just think maybe we'd better stop…"

She'd been staring into his throat when she said that, and now she tilted her head enough to look up into his face. His oh-so-handsome face that she'd come to adore, that held the expression of a man who'd been as lost in what they'd been sharing as she had been.

Before she'd thought about taking off her clothes.

He closed his eyes and arched his eyebrows high. Nina knew he was regrouping. Regaining some control. Even as the heat of his hand still on her flesh made her want him not to.

But then that hand slid away and joined his other one in refastening her bra before they both retreated and ended up flat to the wall on either side of her head.

He dipped down to kiss her again. A long, lingering, openmouthed, seductive kiss that made her have some very serious second thoughts.

Until he ended that kiss, too, and pushed away from her with a finality that said he was honoring her wishes, regardless of how difficult it might be for him.

Then he picked up the bag that held his purchases, took a deep breath and said, "I kind of need you to stay right where you are and let me go upstairs, put on my coat and get the hell out of here. Otherwise I'm not gonna to be able to go at all because there isn't a damn thing I've ever wanted *not* to do as much as leave you right now. Okay?"

"Okay," Nina agreed breathlessly.

"But I'll be back tomorrow night to pick you up for dinner."

Nina muttered another "Okay."

"And thanks," he added. "For the after-hours shopping, for thinking of the boys and for wrapping their shirts." He grinned at her—a grin that turned her knees to mush because he looked so good and sexy and mischievous, and just so Dallas. "And I'd say thanks for sending me home before we did something we might regret, except I just don't think I would have regretted it."

Then he turned and went up the stairs.

Nina watched him go, drinking in every bit of the sight of him climbing those steps, until he reached the top and she couldn't see him anymore.

Only then did she drop her head back to the wall and close her eyes, trying to tell her body that it was for the best that she hadn't let things go any further than they had.

But really, she didn't care what her reasons were.

She just wanted him back there.

She wanted his hands on her again.

And she wanted a whole lot more that she'd left herself only able to have in her imagination....

Chapter 9

Nina was nervous about spending Christmas Eve with the Traubs and considered begging off at the last minute.

But such a big part of her wanted to be with Dallas that she couldn't make herself do that.

Then Dallas came to pick her up, and one look at him sent any idea of not going right out the window.

He looked terrific in charcoal-gray slacks and a lighter gray turtleneck sweater that hugged every well-honed inch of those broad shoulders, pectorals and biceps that she re-membered so vividly having her hands all over the night before. And there was no way she could deny herself being with him.

"Wow! Look at you—you look fabulous!" he complimented her when he first set eyes on her.

She'd changed outfits four times, so she was gratified that he approved. She was wearing the simplest of sweaters—a soft black cocoon of cashmere with long sleeves.

It was the cut of it that made it special. It was tighter at the bottom, the hem reaching to midthigh, giving it a sexy swing. And the fact that the bateau neckline went from the very end of one shoulder to the very end of the other gave it a sexy allure that also kept the focus above the waist.

Under the sweater she wore black leather slim-leg pants with a pair of four-inch heel shoes that dipped enough in front to show just a hint of toe cleavage, so the pants and shoes were also hardly matronly.

But as happy as she was to see Dallas's genuine approval of how she looked—along with a glint of desire in his eyes—she continued to be nervous.

"Are you sure all of your family is going to be okay with having me there?" she fretted on the drive to the Triple T ranch.

"When Ellie Traub gives her stamp of approval to someone it goes a long way with the whole lot of us. And her personal invitation counts as that stamp of approval, so you don't have anything to worry about," Dallas assured her.

But somehow that didn't help as Nina thought about the years and years—actually the full decades and generations—that had gone into the feud between the Crawfords and the Traubs. About the ugly words and accusations that had been flung during the campaign for mayor.

And when she added to that her own inside knowledge of how the Crawfords thought and felt about the Traubs—and had to assume that the Traubs thought and felt the same way about her and the rest of her family—it wasn't easy to believe that a simple invitation was enough to override everything else.

Dallas must have seen her lingering doubts because he cast her a supportive smile and said, "Plus, this Christmas Eve is a little different than usual. It's more of an open house tonight, and Mom is expecting a pretty big crowd. One way or another, though, I promise I'll be right by your side every minute. If at any point you want out, all you have to do is elbow me in the ribs and I'll get it done before you can blink twice. Okay?"

"Okay," Nina agreed, continuing to fret nonetheless.

But it was all for naught.

Dallas hadn't exaggerated when he'd said his mother was expecting a crowd. The large Traub family home was filled to the brim with people—many of whom Nina recognized as mutual friends and neighbors who continued to be in need this year, due to the flood.

It made the Traubs' Christmas Eve an elaborate party, and while Nina was glad for the opportunity to get lost in that sea of guests, she had to admit that the party itself was a nice thing to do for those whose Christmas Eve might not have been so festive otherwise.

And it proved what she'd begun to think about the Traubs before this—that the family she'd been taught to demonize was, instead, much like her own family—people who cared about the misfortune that had fallen on some Rust Creek Falls citizens worse than on others and who wanted to do whatever they could to make things better.

The house was decorated to the hilt, with the dining room table set buffet-style and laden with food. There were hams and turkeys and pork roasts and pasta dishes. There were green salads, fruit salads and macaroni salads, mashed potatoes, scalloped potatoes, macaroni and cheese, and oyster stuffing. There was asparagus and green-bean casserole and sweet potatoes and candied yams. There was hollandaise for the ham, and gravies for the turkeys, the mashed potatoes and the pork roasts. There were pies and cakes and cheesecakes and Christmas cookies and fudge for every sweet tooth. And there were drinks galore, too—soda and punch and wine and beer and eggnog—spiked and unspiked.

Regardless of what troubles might have been hanging on for anyone, they seemed to be suspended for the time being in smiles and laughter as folks mingled and talked and ate of the plentiful food. Dallas's three sons and a number of other children dressed in party clothes ran around and played and let out some of their pent-up excitement over the holiday.

One by one, each of the Traubs made their way to Nina and Dallas, and there was no rancor to be found in any of the encounters. Instead, Nina was welcomed warmly by Ellie and Bob, and found herself chatting amiably enough with each of Dallas's five brothers at one point or another.

His brother Forrest and Forrest's fiancée, Angie, were in from Thunder Canyon, and so was Clay, along with his wife, Antonia, and their two children, her baby daughter, Lucy, and his slightly older son, Bennett.

Of course Collin Traub and his wife, Willa, were there. Collin, the new mayor, was polite, but it was Willa who actually did the talking while they shared an eggnog with Dallas and Nina.

The still-single Braden even came up to say hello and tell Nina he was glad she could make it. And Sutter and his fiancée, Paige, stayed to talk quite a while, with Paige seeming overly interested in Nina's pregnancy.

The entire evening was so amiable that, as it wore on, Nina began to wonder if anyone there even remembered that she was a Crawford. And she certainly had yet another occasion to forget that the Traubs were supposed to be her sworn enemies.

It was nearly ten o'clock before the crowd thinned. While the rest of the family helped Ellie and Bob clean up, Dallas enlisted Nina to join him in getting his boys upstairs to bed.

"Not *home* to bed?" she asked quietly.

"Everybody's spending the night here so we can have one big Christmas morning. We thought maybe if we did it that way it might keep the boys from thinking too much about being without their mother this year."

"Ah…" Nina said in understanding, happy for Ryder, Jake and Robbie that their family all cared so much for them that they were willing to do that.

"Besides," Dallas added with a mischievous smile. "I still have some things to get ready at my house—a bike to finish assembling and some packages that need to be wrapped. Since you're so good at that—" his smile turned into an incorrigible grin "—I thought maybe I could talk you into lending me a hand before I take you back to your place."

"You're going to make me work for my supper?"

"Just a little. If you wouldn't mind…"

As pleasant as the evening had been—and even though Dallas had been true to his word and stayed by her side throughout —it didn't seem as if they'd had much alone time. And while Nina knew—especially after the way the previous evening had ended—that she shouldn't have any alone time with Dallas, when it was suddenly right there for the taking, she couldn't make herself not take it.

So she said, "I don't mind." Which was, in fact, an enormous understatement.

Because the prospect of that alone time had just made her whole night.

"That quiet sounds pretty good, doesn't it?" Dallas commented as he let himself and Nina into his house after they'd gotten Ryder, Jake and Robbie to bed at their grandparents' place and said good-night to the rest of the Traubs.

"Oh, yeah," Nina agreed, not having realized until now the level of noise they'd been in through the party, especially with so many family members remaining to stay overnight. But they were alone at Dallas's place.

Alone with a half-assembled bicycle and several toys waiting to be wrapped.

It was already late, so they wasted no time getting to work—Dallas in the middle of the family room floor and Nina at the kitchen table—after kicking off the shoes that she'd been standing in too long tonight.

"Visions of Christmas future," Dallas said as they went about their separate tasks.

Nina's first thought was that he meant that tonight was her glimpse of future Christmases—with him. And her glance shot to Dallas.

Then she realized he was referring to the many Christmas Eves to come when she'd be assembling toys and wrapping packages for her own child, and she deflated. And relaxed, too, because while there had been the oddest sense of hope in what he'd said, there had also been alarm that he might be suggesting something… Some kind of proposal she didn't want to have to reject…

"I can't wait to tuck in my own little boy or girl and then do this for them," she said to narrow her focus.

"Next Christmas…" Dallas said unnecessarily.

Next Christmas she would have her own child. An almost one-year-old.

It seemed so strange….

And wonderful, too.

It was just difficult to imagine that by this time next year so much would be different. She would have delivered the baby and would know that baby well. Son or daughter. *Her* son or daughter. And so many stages of babydom and parenting would already be past.

"Will I be sorry that the year has gone by, or glad?" she wondered out loud.

"A little of both," he answered, as the voice of experience. "You won't be sorry for getting full nights of sleep again. And you'll be an old hand at diapering and feeding and baths and washing hair—that's an improvement over the first few times when you'll be all thumbs. You'll know hungry cries from fussy cries, tired cries from cries that are just temper and cries that mean you better come quick—that helps. But you'll also look back and feel sad that some things are over and done with."

"It's so weird to think that in just a year's time anything will be over and done with."

"Some things go fast, though. The newborn stage—sure, you're exhausted, but at the same time you get to have this soft little ball of baby in your arms, snuggled there like an angel. You'll have seen a lot of firsts come and go— the first time they hold your finger, the first smile that says they really recognize you, the first time they roll over or sit up or crawl—"

"I guess that's part of why people have more than one—so they can do it all again," Nina mused.

"Part of it, yeah," he agreed. "Do you have plans for that? More artificial insemination for more babies…?"

Why did it sound as if he might care what the answer to that was?

Nina wasn't quite sure, so she merely answered honestly. "No, no plans. What about you? Do you want more kids?"

And why did *she* care what *his* answer might be?

She didn't know. She just knew that if he said he didn't want any more it was going to bother her....

"Three kids doesn't seem like so many when you come from a family with six. And this is a big house—it could handle a couple more. So I guess I wouldn't rule anything out."

Nina smiled without meaning to.

"How about Rust Creek?" he asked then. "Could you see yourself leaving here?"

"No," Nina responded without having to think about it. "I love it here. I love small-town living. The store. Knowing almost everyone—"

"Yeah, but you're only twenty-five. A lot can change between your twenties and your thirties..." he mused, sounding slightly melancholy, so Nina knew he was thinking of his ex-wife's change of heart.

It also served as a reminder to her, though. The more she learned about Dallas the more she found that they had in common and the less aware she was of their age difference.

But that gap never narrowed, and she knew she needed not to forget about it.

"What about you?" she asked. "Could you see yourself leaving here?"

"Not me. Never. My roots here are deep," he said, also without pause.

"And you're set in your ways…" she teased, only to reinforce the reminder that he was so much older than she was. Like Leo, who had used the set-in-his-ways excuse for so much….

But Dallas heard her and laughed. "Go ahead and have that baby—see how set in your ways you get to be once it's here," he challenged. "You'll be in a state of change to meet every change that kid makes from now until…well, I was going to say from now until it goes to college, but come to think of it, not even my folks have the luxury of being set in their ways. Not with the six of us getting engaged and married and bringing kids of our own around. And then if divorce rears its ugly head? That shook things up for them, too, believe me. I don't think they know what's coming at them from one day to the next. I know I don't."

And he adapted to everything he needed to adapt to…*unlike* Leo.

But she was trying hard to remind herself why she needed to resist her attraction to him—why she needed to resist him—and finding him *unlike* Leo didn't help matters.

And she *was* trying to resist what she was feeling for Dallas.

Because, despite so many people being around them tonight at his parents' party, despite the half-a-room distance that separated them now, there still hadn't been a single moment tonight when she hadn't been ultra-aware of him. When she hadn't glanced at him and been struck by how handsome he was. When she hadn't wanted to have her hands on him. Or his hands on her...

Actually there hadn't been a moment since she'd stopped things between them last night that her body had seemed to calm down, to stop craving going right back to what had happened between them and letting it find a conclusion.

A conclusion that was beginning to seem like the only way to get what he'd stirred up in her to die down again....

"In case no one has told you yet," Dallas said then, grinning as if he knew something she didn't. "Once that baby gets here, your life as you've known it will be *forever* changed and changing. Kiss what you've known goodbye, darlin'," he joked. "And embrace whatever comes your way because you'll never know what's next, and there's no use fighting it."

Kissing and embracing…

She heard what he'd said and knew what he was talking about, but those two words really rang in her ears. Because they were what she really wanted to be doing at that moment.

She'd finished the last of the wrapping, so she didn't even have that to do to keep her hands busy.

Or to keep her distance from Dallas.

She went around the island and crossed to him, standing slightly behind him to survey his work.

"Done?" he asked.

"I am."

"Me, too. Just about…"

He gave a few more turns of a screwdriver and sat back on his haunches. "There! I'm getting to be a bike-assembling master!"

"You've done this before," Nina said even though she wasn't looking at the bicycle anymore but at his hair. Not too long. Not too short. Carelessly combed. Clean and shiny and sexy…

She wanted to bury her face in it.

That wasn't something she'd ever considered doing before.

Oh, she just had it so bad for this man!

And it was getting worse by the minute.

All on its own her hand went to his head, smoothing his hair.

But at least not burying her face in it...

Dallas froze.

Then he flipped down the bicycle's kickstand and set the bike upright before he took her hand from his head, stood and turned to face her, releasing her hand the moment he was.

He inhaled noticeably and sighed, looking raptly at her. And, with only two fingers that never actually touched her skin, he raised her sweater's neckline from where it had fallen off her left shoulder and gave it a more demure positioning.

"What're you doing, lady?" he asked, his voice raspy.

Nina shrugged. She couldn't give him any other answer because she wasn't completely sure *what* she was doing. Being carried away, she guessed.

All she knew with any certainty was that her body was screaming for him. It had been for the past twenty-four hours. And while this was certainly not an ideal time for her to enter into anything with Dallas or anyone else, she'd never been in the throes of a desire so persistent, so undeniable, so intense.

A desire he'd said last night that he didn't think he would regret satisfying.

Sounding accepting—reluctantly—he said, "I get that you might not be so interested in…" He obviously wasn't sure how to say *having sex,* but the involuntary glance down at breasts that were contained by a strapless bra tonight made it clear what was on his mind.

And she could only smile at how wrong he was.

"But, Nina," he went on in a tone that rang with frustration. "I want you in the worst way, and if you come any closer or so much as lay another hand on me… I'm gonna bust wide-open."

"That sounds painful," she said in a voice that was pure seductress. She raised a hand to mold to the side of that sculpted face and looked into his blue eyes. "What if I want you in the worst way, too?" she whispered, then glanced at her protruding belly and back at him. "This wouldn't bother you?"

"No," he said with a wry laugh that left no doubt it wasn't an issue for him at all. "But you…last night…"

"Yeah… It made me feel a little…shy…"

she confessed. "But that hasn't seemed to… quench anything."

He laughed, then reiterated what he'd said the night before. "You are amazingly beautiful. That baby bump is nothing but—" he took a turn at shrugging "—nature at work. It doesn't make me want you any less."

He leaned forward and kissed her, as if to prove that. A hopeful kiss that was tentative, too, as if he was afraid of getting where they'd been the night before and then having her pull the plug again.

But there was some kind of something— something indescribable, something almost magical—in whatever it was that was between them. Because all it took was him moving only those inches nearer. All it took was getting one whiff of his cologne. All it took was that simple press of his lips to hers, and to Nina nothing mattered as much as he did. As wanting him did. As getting to have him did…

Just this once, a little voice in the back of her mind rationalized.

Just this once because there were too many reasons why it couldn't be anything *but* this once.

But just this once, as her Christmas gift to herself.

Because she couldn't resist anymore…

She placed a hand on the side of his neck and let her lips part to invite more of that kiss, and Dallas followed suit.

A sound rumbled in his throat, and even without words Nina knew what it meant. He did want her, and his resistance was down, too, so he had to trust that she really would go through with it tonight.

But Nina had every intention of it. There was no way the needs coursing through her would allow anything less.

All tentativeness evaporated from that kiss then, as it grew more fervent, and hunger was unleashed.

Dallas's arms circled her, pulling her to him as his mouth opened wide over hers and his tongue really came to play.

At least for a little while, until it ended and he took her hand. "You're sure?" he asked, giving her one last chance to opt out.

"I'm sure if you are," she told him. "And if you know how it's done at this stage…" she added, a bit insecure about the fact that she didn't have a clue.

He grinned. "I do," he said confidently before he took her upstairs to his room.

It was a big master bedroom and so clean

that Nina had the fleeting thought that he must have expected this tonight—or at least held out hope.

He didn't turn on any lights. Instead, he left the room in only the white glow of a full moon reflected off the snow outside and coming in through large windows exposed by open curtains.

Then he spun her around to face him again at the foot of his king-size bed and recaptured her mouth with his in a kiss that held nothing back now. Instead it started very much where they'd left off the previous night, as if his own needs and desires had been simmering barely beneath the surface since then, too, waiting to be unleashed.

Feverish—that was what that kiss was. Hot and intense and burning bright. And it was everything Nina had been dying for since she'd stopped him from kissing her like that in the store.

He cradled her head in his left hand and braced her back with his right as mouths reclaimed each other and Nina realized she now had free rein...

She slipped her hands under his sweater to his bare back, drinking in the feel of sleek skin over massive muscles. She was up to his shoulders when the thought struck that she didn't have to leave him dressed, and so she tore away from the kiss long enough to pull his sweater off over his head.

He smiled and went right back to kissing her, letting her have her way, exploring him.

And now that she had the chance, Nina didn't leave anything unexplored. She sent her palms on a quest that went from his narrow waist, expanding from there to broad, broad shoulders that she dug her fingers into just a little. She went to biceps that were cut and carved, squeezing those, too, reveling in the feel of power and strength there. And then there were his pectorals and the tiny male nibs that were almost as hard as she could feel her own nipples growing even as she discovered his.

Apparently Dallas decided to continue what she'd begun because he reached down to the very bottom of her sweater and went under, too. But rather than what she'd expected—and hoped for—rather than returning to breasts that were yearning for his attention, he found the waistband of her leather pants and slid them down.

Ah, the advantage of an easy-off waistband…because down they went without incident. Nina kicked them aside and was left in the lacy string bikini panties she'd chosen tonight just because they were comfortable and not because she'd had this in mind as an endgame.

Or so she told herself.

Her sweater had fallen so far down her right arm that the part of her breast that swelled above the strapless bra was exposed. It made her feel sexy and bold. So she let her hands glide from Dallas's chest to his washboard abs. All the way down to the waistband of his slacks.

He really did want her, and that made her smile beneath the onslaught of the kissing that was still going on, and growing hotter and hotter with every passing moment.

And she wanted him to be free to want her....

So she unfastened the hook that held his waistband closed and then unzipped his pants with the help of his own burgeoning needs.

It was such a turn-on to have the evidence of how much he really did yearn for her that Nina felt her own desire take a leap to another level even as she closed her hand around the steely length of him.

He groaned from deep in his throat, and

that was when one of his hands slid under her sweater again. Up the back, he went straight for the hook of her bra, undoing it and then pulling it out to drop on the floor.

Then he did two things at once. He abandoned her mouth and nuzzled the top of her sweater to dip low enough to expose one breast to his seeking mouth as his hand found the other breast from inside the sweater.

And suddenly there was so much that was so deliciously sweet all at once…

He kneaded and massaged and toyed with her nipple while sucking the other breast deeply into the warm, wet velvet of his mouth, flicking the crest with the tip of his tongue, nipping with tender teeth and giving Nina her reason for moaning.

It all felt so divine that her spine arched and let him know she just wanted more. More and more and more, and maybe nothing would be enough when she wanted him as much as she did.

His other hand located the string of her panties and he disposed of those, too, bringing his hand back to the side of what used to be her waist. And just like that, mounting desire mingled just a bit with self-consciousness.

But his hand was big and warm, and so, so adept, too, and the way he slid it to the underside of her belly—gently, lovingly, adoringly—dissolved some of the awkwardness.

Just before he slipped lower still and his hand ended up between her legs...

The gasp at that first touch took her by surprise, and when his fingers slipped into her she very nearly turned to mush. Her knees actually did weaken enough for her to rely more on leaning into Dallas's big body, and her grip around him tightened, too, apparently giving him the signal that it was time to get her off her feet.

But not without getting rid of her sweater first.

He returned to kissing her after he did that, giving her a deep, poignant kiss laced with so much passion that it was the sexiest kiss she'd ever had, and it washed away every last reservation about being naked with him.

Then he scooped her up into his arms much the way he had that day in the blizzard—only so much better this time—and he laid her on his bed, joining her there.

That was when the urgency that had been growing in Nina since the night before burst to the surface. And apparently the same thing happened for Dallas because a new concentration, a new intensity, came to everything then. To his mouth at her breasts, to his hands all over her body, to her hands all over him...

Until she knew she couldn't last much longer, not without the full feel of him inside her. Not without the release that her body was beyond needing...

Then he wasn't lying facing her anymore, he was behind her, spooning her, kissing her shoulder, flicking his tongue there. One hand still worked its magic at her breasts and the other shifted her legs just so, freeing a way for him to find his home right where she craved him to be.

Part surprise, part sigh, part moan was what sounded from her then as he taught her the delights of a position she'd never known before. He moved carefully into her and retreated, carefully in even more, all the while continuing to arouse with the wonders of his hands on her, giving her nipples his palms to kernel ever more tightly into, kneading and taking her on a ride that was so incredibly not set in its way that she didn't know what to do but let him take her on it.

And take her on it he did. Coming deeply and more deeply into her. Delving gently, carefully, but still faster and faster into the core of her, building white-hot flames to burn and fuel her. To drive her higher and higher, striving for that peak that he seemed to know exactly when to bring.

Because just when she was desperate for it, one hand deserted her breasts and reached down below instead…

He definitely knew what he was doing because he sent her right over the top into a climax so incredible she lost herself in it. In it, and in that man and what he was doing to her, even as she felt him plunge into her and shudder with a culmination of his own that made him catch his breath, too, and kept them both suspended in pure, exquisite ecstasy…

Then Dallas melded his body around hers so seamlessly it was as if they were two pieces of clay formed to fit together.

He kissed her shoulder once more. "You okay?" he asked in a gravelly voice.

"Wow…" was all she could whisper in response as she slowly came back to her senses.

"But are you okay…?" he asked again.

"Oh, yeah. Better than that…"

He laughed a relieved, replete laugh and placed a trail of kisses along the length of her shoulder and up the side of her neck before he laid his head on the mattress above hers, making a nest for her head under his chin.

They stayed that way for a while before Nina recalled that it was Christmas Eve. That even though she'd accepted his mother's invitation to Christmas dinner the next day because her own family continued to be quarantined, Dallas still needed to have Christmas morning with his boys, with his family.

"You have to get me home," she reminded him softly.

"I don't want you to *go* home," he said.

"I don't want to go home," she commiserated with a laugh. "But I have to. I don't think me and my being here in the same clothes I wore tonight is quite what anyone is expecting Santa to bring."

He laughed. "It's what *I* want Santa to bring," he insisted.

But then he sighed in resignation, kissed the top of her head and said, "I know, I know…" And he did the last thing Nina wanted him to do—he took his arms from where they were wrapped so warmly around her, he took the long, heavy leg he had locked over her hips away, and he got up to retrieve their clothes.

He brought her hers first, unashamedly giving her a pretty terrific Christmas gift in the view of his magnificent body naked in the moonlight. Then he sat on the end of the bed and put his own clothes on with his back to her.

Nina appreciated that and wasted no time dressing herself, not really eager to give him the same unfettered view of her.

And once they were both decent again, Dallas came to her to kiss her once more— a long, leisurely, sexy kiss that only made it more difficult to go out into the cold night for the drive back to her apartment.

A long, leisurely, sexy kiss that was probably the reason that, once they got there and he gave her another one, he didn't end up leaving her at her door.

Instead Nina did what she'd been sorry she hadn't done the previous night.

She took him to her bed.

For just one more time…

Chapter 10

After his night with Nina, and slipping into his parents' house at three in the morning, and very few hours of rest after that, Dallas was still the first one up on Christmas morning. Mainly because he was just too elated to sleep much.

He lit the Christmas tree lights and a fire in the fireplace. He sorted all the gifts into piles specific to each person. And he was humming Christmas carols as he made coffee in the kitchen, feeling better than he had in longer than he could remember. Maybe since soon after Robbie was born, when he'd given up thinking that anything was going to please Laurel.

And it was all because of Nina.

"Merry Christmas," a sleepy-sounding Ryder said from behind him.

Dallas glanced over his shoulder to see his oldest son standing in the doorway in his flannel pajamas, surprised that it was Ryder who was first to rise and not Robbie.

"Merry Christmas!" Dallas answered. "Anybody else up?"

"Just me," Ryder informed him.

"Did you check out the presents?"

"Mmm, a little," Ryder said, as if he wasn't sure it was all right if he had. "I saw a base-ball mitt…"

One of the things he'd asked for.

"…and that swamp creature Jake wanted and Robbie's bike."

Those were the gifts left unwrapped, as if Santa had set them out.

"I hope Robbie got the deluxe neon alien invasion spaceship, too," Ryder added with a hint of warning, as if Dallas might have overlooked the toy the youngest of the Traub sons had asked for repeatedly—and without omitting a single word of the lengthy description.

"I don't think he'll be disappointed," Dallas said, silently thanking Paige for that contribution early on, when he'd still been too muddled in his own misery to be paying as much attention as he should have been to what his kids were saying.

Sutter had spent a lot of time in Rust Creek Falls in November and had done some babysitting for him. The boys had gone along several times to do things with Paige, such as make cookies and help sort food for the food drives.

Paige had also helped Robbie write a letter to Santa asking for his mom to come back. Or, if he couldn't have that, then a new mom. Or, if he couldn't have that, then a deluxe neon alien invasion spaceship.

Dallas had been more stuck on the mom issue, but Paige had kept the spaceship in mind and picked one of the season's hot items up when she'd had the opportunity. By the time Dallas had even begun to think about gifts, it likely would have been too late to get one at all, which would have disappointed his youngest.

The alien spaceship was in one of the wrapped packages from Santa—Paige hadn't even wanted the credit—and Dallas made a mental note to thank her again for that kindness and consideration.

He just had to hope that the spaceship was enough to compensate for Robbie's other requests not being met because there was no mom—new or old—under that tree.

Ryder came to stand beside him. "I like the way coffee smells, but it tastes like licking a dirty ashtray."

"When have you ever licked a dirty ashtray?" Dallas asked with a smile.

"You know, I just think it's what it would taste like. Yuck."

"Well you're a little young for coffee yet, so it's probably better that you don't like the taste of it. How about some juice while we wait for everyone else to get up?"

Ryder shrugged his concession to that.

"Your grandmother has a big breakfast planned for after we open gifts but I don't think anybody would notice if we hit that cookie tray," Dallas suggested.

Ryder reached far back on the counter for the tray of Christmas goodies and slid it forward while Dallas poured his juice.

As they ate iced cut-out cookies, Ryder said, "This has been a pretty good Christmas."

He sounded surprised by that, which confirmed what had seemed to be the case—that the ten-year-old hadn't been looking forward to this holiday. Understandable, under the circumstances.

"It was tomorrow when Mom left last year," Ryder said then, as if Dallas might not realize that.

"I know," Dallas said.

"And her not bein' here this year made it kind of…not much fun…"

"I know," Dallas repeated sympathetically. "It's hard. I know you guys miss her."

"Do you?"

"I did," Dallas confided. "Then I just got pretty sad. And mad. And in kind of a bad mood I couldn't get out of."

Ryder nodded his head knowingly. "But Nina made some of the things better. It was fun when she brought the Christmas tree and helped decorate it. And the rest of the stuff we did with her. She's, like…you know, kind of happier than Mom was."

Dallas wasn't sure what to say to that. Should he talk about Laurel's unhappiness and discontent with her life? Should he explain that Ryder and Jake and Robbie weren't to blame? Should he get into all of that now, on Christmas morning?

It just didn't seem as though he should. It was a subject he obviously needed to address, but not right there and then. And likely not with Ryder alone.

So he said, "Yeah, I think Nina is a happier person than your mom. Some people are, you know? We're all just different—look at you and Jake and Robbie. There are things about you that are the same but there's a lot about you that's different from your brothers."

"I don't play jokes like Jake, and Robbie's a baby," Ryder summed up the only differences he seemed to see.

"Well, that's one way to look at it. But maybe because you're closer to being a man you take things more seriously, too. That could make you seem a little less happy than Jake or a little more mature than Robbie," Dallas offered, hoping to put some sort of positive spin on Ryder's introversion and his more obvious sorrow at the loss of his mother.

Ryder shrugged. "We all like Nina, though," he said. "When she's around... I don't know, I guess maybe because she's happier than Mom was, we're happier then, too."

"I know she makes me feel better," Dallas admitted, realizing just how true that was. How true it had been since that day in the blizzard. "But I'm glad to hear that she makes you guys feel better, too."

"I think Robbie wants her to be our new mom," Ryder said as if he wasn't sure he should say that, the same way he hadn't been sure he should say he'd looked at the presents around the tree.

"I don't think moms are like shoes—you don't just get new ones."

"Yeah. But you can get second ones. Lots of kids have stepmoms or stepdads—that's what those are. Like Uncle Clay and Aunt Antonia—Uncle Clay is Lucy's stepfather and Aunt Antonia is Bennett's stepmom," he explained, as if Dallas had somehow missed that fact. "But they're a real family."

"True," Dallas said.

"Maybe Nina might not be so bad for that."

High praise coming from Ryder.

And for some reason, Dallas appreciated that stamp of approval.

But all he did was ruffle his son's hair and say, "Well, today is Christmas and let's just enjoy that for now, huh?"

"Yeah," Ryder agreed, showing some restrained enthusiasm."

Robbie charged into the kitchen just then. "There you guys are! Santa came! When can we open presents?"

"We have to wait—"

"No more waiting," Ellie Traub said wearily, coming up behind Robbie. "He has us all up. Just pour out cups of that coffee I smell, and we can get this show on the road."

Christmas morning was the best kind of chaos. It was a houseful of family injected with the delight of children—Dallas's three boys, and his brother Clay's small son, Bennett, and Clay's stepdaughter, baby Lucy.

After the melee of gift opening Dallas's mother headed up breakfast preparations, putting everyone to work.

Dallas sneaked away then to call Nina, to wish her a Merry Christmas and make sure she was doing all right, that there hadn't been any ill-effects from their night together.

Just as she was assuring him she was fine, Jake found him and Dallas was forced to cut the call short.

"It's okay. *I'm* okay," Nina said. "Go and have Christmas morning with your boys!"

"I'll see you soon," he said, thinking that it couldn't be soon enough.

"See you soon," Nina echoed, and he thought she just might sound as if she felt the same way.

When it was ready, breakfast was shared with everyone sitting around the expanded dining room table.

Disagreements that had arisen between the brothers recently and in times gone by were put aside for the holiday, and breakfast was accompanied by laughing and joking and teasing, and reminiscing about Christmases past in the Traub family.

Even though they'd all been together at Thanksgiving, Dallas knew that a part of why they'd all made sure to come together again for Christmas was for him and the boys, to help distract them from thoughts of Laurel and the anniversary of her leaving. And he appreciated that.

But he also knew that another part of communing over both holidays was that the damage, destruction and disruption caused by Rust Creek's flood had shaken everyone up in one way or another. It had left them all with a need to come together, to regroup and touch home base, to be reassured that there was still that place and those people to go home to.

When breakfast was over and the mess cleaned, everyone went their separate ways to visit other friends and family.

Dallas took the boys and all their gifts home for a few hours of playing with their new things before he oversaw three baths, washed three heads of hair and dispatched his sons to dress for Christmas dinner back at their grandparents' house.

The Christmas dinner that they would go and pick Nina up for...

"Get a move on—no messing around," he commanded his sons, because he felt as though he'd been without her for far, far too long already today, and he couldn't wait to get to her, to see her again, to have her by his side.

He showered, shampooed and shaved to get ready, too, then dressed in a pair of tan corduroy pants and an espresso-colored polo sweater, wishing that there had been a way of including Nina all day long. Because, as good as the day had been, he'd still missed her more than he thought it was possible to miss anyone.

"Come on, boys—I need to see how you look before we go and we *need* to go," he called as he left his own room and headed downstairs.

The sound of his three sons tussling to get out of their shared room and down the steps was familiar. And then there they were in the entryway, dressed in the slacks he'd set out for them.

But none of them had on the sweaters he'd also decided they should wear.

Instead, each of them wore the shirt he'd bought and pretended had come from their mother.

"Oh…" Dallas said when he first saw them.

"We wanted to wear Mom's shirts," Robbie announced proudly.

So they really had needed to believe that she'd thought of them.

It stabbed Dallas through the heart and at the same time made him grateful to Nina for having come up with the idea.

"Is that okay?" Ryder asked, sounding tentative but hopeful.

"Sure it is," Dallas answered without hesitation.

"Ryder says just 'cuz she sent 'em doesn't mean she's comin' back—like it said on the tags," Robbie informed him.

"No, it doesn't," Dallas confirmed.

"But she didn't forget us like we're nothin', either," Jake said.

"You guys are not nothing. You're not nothing at all. You're great kids," Dallas assured them, hating that that's what their mother had caused them to feel and needing to bear hug them all together right then, for his own sake if not for theirs.

They barely suffered his hug before wiggling free.

"And we wanted to look nice for Nina," Robbie added then.

"Yeah, me, too," Dallas said.

"'Cuz she helped us have this Christmas," his youngest pointed out matter-of-factly.

"Yes, she did." And they'd never know to what extent she'd helped them have this Christmas. But something swelled in his heart for her, just the same.

"So let's go get 'er," Jake said, as if he didn't know why they were wasting time.

"Yeah, let's," Dallas said, thinking that, once they did, he wasn't sure how he was going to let go of her again.

Ever.

Nina spoke to her mother on the phone to wish everyone a Merry Christmas. Laura Crawford was still feeling just fine, convinced that she'd had what the rest of the family had the month before, so was at no risk of getting it. But she again told Nina to stay away, assuring her they would have Christmas when the bug was gone.

So Nina spent the day putting the final touches on the nursery. And thinking about

Dallas more than about her coming baby because she was still in the rosy glow of the night they'd spent together.

Once the nursery was in order, she showered and got ready for Christmas dinner with the Traubs.

She wore a black velvet jumper, cut just A-line enough to camouflage what Dallas liked to call her baby bump, over a high-necked white blouse. Black tights and a simple pair of black patent-leather Mary Janes finished the Christmassy and very prim look that belied the not-at-all-prim memories she kept having about the night before. Memories that inspired desire to spring to life again as if it hadn't been quenched, twice.

"Last night was supposed to take care of that," she lectured herself as she brushed out her hair and left it loose, then applied blush, mascara, just a hint of eye shadow and a little lip gloss.

But rather than squelching those cravings for Dallas, being with him had only added fuel to the fire.

And when she heard a knock on the door to her apartment that told her he was there, squelching anything went by the wayside as she rushed just to get to see him again.

"Merry Christmas!" he greeted her for the second time that day when she opened the door.

"Merry Christmas," Nina answered, just as jovially.

Then he produced a sprig of mistletoe from behind his back, held it over her head and grinned.

"We have to behave," she warned, speaking as much to herself as to him.

"I know," he agreed, ignoring it all anyway as he stepped over her threshold, wrapped his nonmistletoe-bearing arm around her to pull her to him and kissed her soundly.

"Now *that's* what I needed," he breathed when the kiss ended. "Well, the beginning of it, anyway. Too bad the boys are down in the truck…"

Or, Nina knew, she and Dallas would have ended up in bed again despite her resolve that last night be their only night together.

And while she told herself this was the perfect opportunity to let him know her intentions, her mind was already wandering to that night.

After dinner.

To the possibility that the boys wouldn't tag along when he brought her home…

Then it wouldn't only be a one-night stand, she reasoned, knowing she was just looking for an excuse.

But they had a dinner to get to and his sons were waiting, and after he kissed her again he let go of her and held her coat for her to slip into.

The ride to the Triple T ranch was filled with all three boys talking about what they'd received for Christmas.

"And these shirts," Robbie pointed out, holding open his coat to display what he was wearing. "Our mom sent 'em to us."

Nina glanced at Dallas, who smiled gratefully at her. Then she said, "Let me see yours, Ryder and Jake."

They showed them off, just as pleased as the youngest Traub had, breaking Nina's heart yet again to see how thrilled they were to have what they believed were gifts from their mother.

"Oh, yeah, those are really nice shirts," she decreed, glad that Robbie moved on right away to telling her about the deluxe neon alien invasion spaceship he'd also received.

"We took all our new stuff to our house, but I brought that back with us so I could show you."

"Oh, good, I've been wanting to see one of those," Nina told him just as they arrived at the elder Traubs' home.

Except for Nina, Christmas dinner was only family, and Dallas's parents and siblings welcomed her once again with open arms.

The meal began with squash soup with a dollop of crème fraiche and a sprinkling of crispy fried pancetta on top. That was followed by a giant prime rib roast, cooked to perfection, garlic mashed potatoes, a mélange of vegetables in butter sauce, a green salad, a fruit ambrosia and homemade rolls.

Dessert was to be a seven-layer chocolate cake, but just as they were getting to that Nina felt a little odd and excused herself to go to the bathroom.

Luckily she made it just in time, so that when her water broke it wasn't on one of the Traub's dining room chairs.

With her pulse racing, she cleaned herself up, then slipped out of the bathroom. Robbie was nearby, and that seemed like a godsend when a surprisingly strong pain began to build.

"Would you go get your dad for me, please?" she managed to ask the little boy before the pain doubled her over.

Dallas was there just as it did. "Uh-oh," he breathed when he saw her leaning against the bathroom door frame.

Nina nodded through the pain, and when it was over she said, "My water broke and I think... I think I'm going to have this baby now."

"No thinking about it, sweetheart. You are."

Nina hadn't thought that she would ever be as grateful to Dallas as she had been through the blizzard. But from the moment of that first contraction, she was.

He took over again the way he had that day and before she knew it, he'd called to tell her family what was happening, and that he would take care of everything, and she was in his truck being raced to the hospital in Kalispell.

Along the way he kept things light, he talked her through pains that were intense, regular and started at ten minutes apart. He joked with her; he reassured her that everything was going to be all right.

And he swore that nothing was going to pry him away from her side until that baby was born.

The tales Nina had heard about many first

babies requiring long hours of labor were the complete opposite of her experience. As soon as they reached the hospital in Kalispell the doctor in the emergency room examined her and she was rushed to a delivery room while the nursing staff hurried Dallas into a surgical gown and booties.

Then he was ushered in to sit at her head, where he kept her hair out of her eyes and helped her raise up when she needed to push, all the while being referred to as "Dad" since there was no chance to explain that he wasn't the father of her baby.

And after hors d'oeuvres at six o'clock, dinner at seven and missing dessert at eight, at 10:10 on Christmas night—gripping Dallas's hand in a bone-crushing grip—Nina delivered a five-pound, nine-ounce healthy baby girl, who brought tears to her mother's eyes the moment her new daughter was placed in her arms.

And, Nina thought, she brought a suspicious glimmer of moisture to Dallas's eyes, too...

Chapter 11

"Good morning, little Noelle," Dallas whispered to the tiny bundle he was holding.

The sun was just coming up on the day after Christmas and he could hear the sounds of the hospital beginning its morning routine.

But inside that room all was quiet.

Nina was sleeping exhaustedly, the way she had been since she'd been taken from delivery to the maternity ward and finally finished what it involved to be admitted and settled into her room.

But when her daughter—whom Nina had spontaneously named Noelle in honor of the Christmas birth—had stirred in her own hospital bassinet beside her mother's bed, Dallas had picked her up, hoping to buy Nina a little more sleep.

Noelle was small, but pink and perfect, with just a smattering of hair the color of Nina's. And gazing down at her made him smile.

"You're a beauty, like your mama," he told her in that same, almost inaudible whisper. "But you must be tired, too, so why don't you go back to sleep for a little while?"

As if obeying, the newborn balled up her fists under her chin, closed her eyes and did just that, making Dallas smile all over again.

But he didn't put her back in her bassinet. He continued to hold her, to look down at her. To marvel at the wonders of new life.

And to feel things for her that he had no right to feel.

Weary and sleep-deprived himself, he glanced at Nina.

Still sleeping. And she *was* a beauty—it struck him all over again.

Actually, it struck him almost every time he looked at her. And what he felt for her washed through him with the force of the flood that had nearly leveled Rust Creek Falls.

He'd told her he would stay by her side through the delivery, but he hadn't left her side yet, despite her telling him he could. And not because he thought it was the right thing to do, like when he'd brought her here after their near-collision in the blizzard.

No, he'd stayed by her side because that was where he wanted to be. So much that nothing could have torn him away from it while Noelle was being born. So much that he couldn't even tear himself away the rest of the night, either. Away from Nina or away from Noelle.

You're not mine....

You're neither one mine, he reminded himself.

But somehow it felt as if they were. Or, at least, as if they should be. And the thought of walking away from either of them was something he just couldn't find it in himself to do.

He let his head rest against the back of the lounger he'd been sitting in for the past few hours. He thought that this might have been the room that Laurel was in when Ryder was born, but unlike being here with Nina after their near collision, that thought didn't disturb him now. Now it was Nina's room, and being there with her seemed so natural that nothing that had come before it could have an impact.

After marveling—and reveling—in that fact for a moment, he closed his eyes the way he had for brief catnaps while watching over these two.

But this time he had no intention of sleeping. This time he tried to mentally remove himself from this picture the way he knew he should.

You already have three kids waiting for you at the ranch. Three kids you need to go home to. Three kids to think of...

And after spending the past year being the voice of reason every time anyone he knew had fallen in love—the voice of doom, some would say—he tried to be the voice of reason again now. With himself.

There was no doubt that Laurel had left him gun-shy when it came to romance, to relationships, to marriage. For himself or for anyone else. It could all just so easily go sour, and no matter how hard a person tried, they couldn't sweeten it up again—it was a harsh lesson he'd learned.

He and Laurel had gotten together so young—that was what he'd decided was the main cause of things not working out between them. That, while he might have known exactly what he wanted, Laurel had been more the child doing what she was told, what was expected of her, what had been fairly easy to persuade her to do. Had she been less the child and more the adult, she might not have made the choices she had. The choices she'd regretted and amended when it had hurt so many.

So he'd decided that if he ever got involved with anyone again—and he hadn't been sure he ever would—the woman would have to be mature and stable. Someone whose feet were firmly planted on the ground.

But Nina was only twenty-five. A single year older than Laurel had been when he'd finally talked her into actually marrying him.

What if, a few years from now when Nina was older, she felt stifled the way Laurel had? What if she woke up one day and decided she wasn't happy living in Rock Creek Falls anymore? What if being a parent turned out to be a trial for her the way it had been for Laurel, and she wanted to push the reset button, too? She could even bail and leave him with *her* daughter....

Trust. That was part of this, Dallas realized.

He knew that while Laurel might not have taken the kids away from him, she had taken away some of his ability to trust. To trust another woman. To trust his own judgment when it came to women.

But then he opened his eyes and looked at Nina again, thinking: *This is Nina. Not Laurel...*

And as he started to actually see Nina, he silently, wryly, chuckled at his own thoughts. At how he'd just portrayed her in his mind. The second Laurel...

It was all a damn scary scene he'd painted.

But it wasn't the real Nina, and he knew it.

No, she didn't have the years on her—there was no denying that. And, yes, her venturing into single parenthood might have seemed a little rash to him at the beginning. But now it served as a sign to him that Nina really did know her own mind. That she really did know what she wanted. And that she was strong enough to make the decision to have this baby on her own, to raise this baby on her own, and to take the steps to accomplish it.

And if anyone could handle single parenthood, it was Nina.

If anyone *would* deal with whatever unforeseen difficulties might come of it, it was Nina.

If anyone would dig in her heels and make it work, it was Nina.

Because young or not, she was still a woman of substance, of grit, of everything good and kind and sweet and generous and giving. And she was about as grounded a person as he'd ever met.

He'd seen her in action, he'd seen with his own two eyes how much she loved Rust Creek Falls and what she was willing to do to help it come back from the flood—even being eight months pregnant. And not only was it impressive, not only were her pure will and determination and energy level impressive, but no one did all she'd done for a place they would leave behind, either.

And he'd also seen what she'd done for him and his boys—she was a problem solver, she was someone who hunkered down and did what needed to be done. Someone who thought enough of family, of kids, to want to help them see light again at the end of the divorce tunnel.

Even when it wasn't her own family.

Even when it was a family her own was feuding with.

None of that—not a single thing—would have been Laurel. Not at any age. Laurel was as Laurel had begun—all about herself.

Laurel, who hadn't sent a thing to the boys to remember them at Christmas.

Instead, it was Nina who had saved Christmas—for him and the boys. Both with what she'd done openly and with what she'd done behind the scenes with those shirts his sons were all so delighted to believe were from their mother.

Nina, who showed no jealousy over Laurel. Who hadn't cared about making the other woman look good or bad. Who had only thought about his boys and that it might make them feel better to allow them to think their mother hadn't completely forgotten them. Hadn't thought they were nothing...

Also unlike Laurel.

No, Nina was nothing like his ex-wife and she wouldn't just turn her back on a husband, a marriage, kids, to run off for her own sake, any more than he would.

But what was he thinking? he asked himself. What was he *really* thinking?

About marriage and Nina?

Well, here you are, a small clear voice in the back of his mind said, *fresh out of her delivery room, holding her daughter, not knowing how you're going to be able to leave either of them behind....*

Marriage and Nina.

Where was that gun-shyness he'd hit everyone else with this past year?

Nowhere to be found.

Because, even though he didn't know how it had happened, he'd somehow fallen in love with Nina.

He hadn't let himself categorize the way he was feeling about her before. But there and then, tired and emotionally raw, his guard was down. And it all worked together to leave bare what those feelings genuinely were.

He loved her. In a way he might not have ever loved Laurel.

What he'd felt for Laurel had begun when they were kids. It had begun as what was probably puppy love. And maybe the fact that they'd gone from there had left a certain amount of *im*maturity to it.

He hadn't realized that before, but now, comparing what he'd felt for Laurel with what he felt for Nina, he could tell the difference.

This was something deeper, more intense, stronger and more resilient. It was the adult version. It was *him,* mature and stable, feet firmly planted on the ground, in love with her.

But what about her?

Yes, she was far beyond Laurel when it came to maturity and stability, and the kind of person she was. But did she feel for him what he felt for her? And even if she did, was she willing to take on someone older than she was again? Was she willing to take on someone who already had three kids of his own?

And what about that damn feud?

He wasn't worried so much about his family—he didn't believe that Christmas had been merely a show. He honestly thought that they were willing to accept Nina—even though she was a Crawford—if she made him happy. And she did.

But what about her family?

There wasn't anything warm and fuzzy on that front. Even the night before, when he'd called to say Nina had gone into labor and that he was taking her to the hospital, her mother had been outraged to learn that Nina was with him.

So, no, that would not be an easy road to travel.

And trying to end the generations-old battle between the Crawfords and the Traubs might be an undertaking bigger than Nina would want to deal with.

But what was it she'd told him at the very start of this whole thing, when she'd talked about using artificial insemination to have this baby?

That sometimes a person had to go after what they wanted.

No matter what, and even if not everything is just right, Dallas added himself.

At least he had to try to go after what he wanted.

Which was Nina.

And Noelle.

And a life with them in Rust Creek Falls...

Nothing had ever looked as good to Nina as the sight of Dallas sitting beside her hospital bed holding her tiny new daughter in his big, muscular arms, against his broad chest.

He was gazing down at Noelle, letting her grasp his index finger in one of her tiny fists, beaming at her with a look of such warmth and delight and adoration in his blue eyes.

For a moment, Nina stayed perfectly still, perfectly quiet, just looking at the two of them, trying to burn the image into her brain to keep forever, and marveling at the pure potency of what she felt at that moment.

Then, as if to check on her, Dallas looked up from the baby and when he saw that Nina was awake, he grinned that one-sided grin of his and said a simple "Hey."

"You didn't go home," Nina responded, marveling at that fact, too. And how glad she was that he hadn't. And how safe and secure it made her feel to have him there.

"Nah, couldn't do it," he said, taking a deep breath that expanded his chest.

He stood and came to sit on the side of her bed with Noelle, facing Nina.

Nina couldn't resist reaching out to touch the baby's hand wrapped so tightly around his finger. And his finger, too...

"How come? Wouldn't your truck start or did we have another blizzard or—"

He shook his head. "I couldn't do it because I couldn't *make* myself do it."

Nina smiled, but only tentatively. He seemed to be getting at something and she was a little afraid of what it might be.

Or maybe afraid to hope what it might be...

Then he started to talk about sitting there with Noelle, about the fact that he hadn't been able to make himself leave either one of them, about that getting him to thinking....

And the sweet, sweet things he said about what he felt for her, what he felt for Noelle, what he wanted, brought tears to Nina's eyes.

"I know we're not the same age and never will be," he said, extracting his finger from the newborn so he could stroke Nina's cheek. "And I know I have three kids I'd be asking you to take on, and that's a lot. And even though my family has let you slip through a crack in their side of the feud, that doesn't necessarily mean they're ready to lay down the hatchet completely—although I have some hopes. And your family still hates the idea of anything Traub, but—"

He paused, shook his head and shrugged as if none of that really mattered. "I love you, Nina. I love you so much I'm bowled over by it. I want to move you and this baby into my house before you ever get out of this bed so you both can come home with me when you leave here. I want a whole lifetime with you, with Noelle, that starts right now. I want you to go on looking out for my boys and making their lives better. I even want a couple more of these—" he jiggled Noelle ever so slightly "—that we make ourselves. And I can't leave until I know there's any chance that I might be able to have—"

"Nina!"

"You. To have it all with you," Dallas finished despite the hushed but harsh voice of Laura Crawford coming from behind him, from where Nina's mother stood in the doorway.

"Mom," Nina greeted quietly. "I didn't think you would be able to come…"

Nina had been completely tuned in to Dallas and what he was saying. And his broad shoulders effectively blocked the view of the doorway, so there had been no indication that her mother was standing there or for how long or how much she might have overheard. But apparently it was enough.

"I called the hospital before dawn and talked to them about whether or not I could come over here from a sick house. They said as long as I wasn't sick and I wore this getup and this mask and didn't touch the baby, they'd let me in. I thought you'd be alone…"

Even standing there looking like a green marshmallow, a surgical mask covering her nose and mouth, her mother still managed to convey righteous indignation. Quiet righteous indignation, but still righteous indignation.

"No, Dallas has been with me the whole time," Nina said, infusing her words with a plea to be reasonable.

"And now he wants to move you into his house? He wants to take over my grandbaby?"

So she'd heard plenty. Nina wasn't ready to get into any of that with her yet so she merely said, "Did you come to see your granddaughter or to fight?"

"I didn't come to see her in the hands of a

Traub," Laura Crawford muttered under her breath, just loudly enough to be heard.

Nina shook her head disgustedly but said to Dallas, "Maybe you could give us a minute. And take the baby to the nursery, where she doesn't have to be in the middle of this."

"I'll do whatever you want," Dallas assured her.

He took Noelle to the doorway Laura Crawford continued to block, and stood tall and strong and unyielding in front of her when he said, "Mrs. Crawford, this is your granddaughter. I know you have to want a look no matter who's holding her...."

Laura cast him another scathing glare from over the surgical mask and gazed down at Noelle, her eyes filling with tears at that first glimpse of the newborn, despite whatever anger she felt at Dallas.

"Beautiful, isn't she?" Dallas asked calmly, understandingly.

Then he said, "I love your daughter, Mrs. Crawford. I already love this little girl here in my arms. I just want the chance to make Nina as happy as she makes me. I want to look out for her daughter the way she's looked out for my boys, and I want to make a life for us all. Can't we put the rest behind us?"

Nina watched her mother blink back her tears over seeing Noelle for the first time but stubbornly say nothing in response to Dallas. Instead, she stepped aside so he could take the baby out.

Over his shoulder, Dallas cast Nina a glance that asked if she was sure she wanted him to go. And only when Nina nodded in response did he finally disappear down the corridor with Noelle.

Nina raised the head of her bed so she could sit more upright to face what she knew was coming as her mother crossed the room.

"I can't believe this," her mother said despondently, going on to voice her disapproval in no uncertain terms.

But Nina couldn't concentrate on her mother's hushed-for-the-hospital tirade. She was still thinking too much about what Dallas had just said.

He loved her.

He loved her.

He *loved* her…

And still awash in all that had filled her own heart when she'd opened her eyes to see him holding Noelle, it struck her like a bolt of lightning that she loved him, too.

But clearly it wasn't that simple.

Not when she was under the attack of her mother's dislike of the Traubs.

Not when she was envisioning being uprooted from her apartment, taking Noelle home to Dallas's house rather than to the nursery Nina had made for her, *moving* out to Dallas's ranch and stepping into his already established life and family. Not when she was envisioning all the adapting and accommodating that that meant for her.

All the adapting and accommodating that was so much like what she'd had to do for Leo and had sworn to herself that she wouldn't do again for another man. That she would only do for Noelle.

Noelle, who was her first priority, the one she had to think about now.

Wouldn't saying yes to Dallas cause her hours-old daughter to take a backseat? Rather than being the coveted first and only child, the way she'd come into this world, she would instantly be just one of *four* kids. Was that fair to her?

Nina's mind was spinning faster than her mother was talking.

She'd planned to devote herself to this baby she'd wanted so much. She fully intended to dote on Noelle, and she already loved her like she'd never loved anything or anyone. And no, the idea of Noelle taking a backseat to anything or anybody did not appeal to Nina.

But when she thought about the expression on Dallas's handsome face when she'd first opened her eyes to that sight of him holding Noelle such a short while ago, she realized that she'd seen the doting and all she felt for Noelle coming from him, too. Which meant that Noelle could have *two* loving, adoring, doting parents instead of just one.

And when she thought of it that way, it felt a little like she would be denying her daughter something if Nina said no.

But Noelle would still be one of *four* kids.

And Nina couldn't bear to think of her daughter lost in the shuffle.

On the other hand, Nina herself had been the youngest of six and she'd never felt lost in any shuffle.

Instead she'd always had someone to play with, to follow around and torment to amuse herself. She'd always had someone whose bed she could crawl into if she had a nightmare. She'd never been alone in facing bullies or the trials and tribulations of growing up. She'd had brothers and a sister to turn to for comfort after the breakup with Leo. She wasn't alone in dealing with her parents aging, and when she lost her parents, she wouldn't be left alone in the world then, either.

Because she had family.

Yes, there had been some adapting to be done in that family. But they'd adapted to her as much as she'd had to adapt to anyone else. It had only been with Leo that she had found herself needing to be the only one in the relationship to accommodate.

And now that she thought about it, it occurred to her that Leo had been an only child. Maybe that was why he hadn't learned to do anything other than expect someone else to meet his needs while putting their own on the back burner. Maybe that had contributed to his expectations that she be flexible while he insisted on remaining a creature of habit. Maybe it hadn't been just the age difference that had put her at a disadvantage.

But Dallas came from the same kind of upbringing she did. From a big family. And, yes, he was older than she was—almost as much older as Leo had been. But he was a kind, caring, generous, compassionate man who had sacrificed himself more than once to step in and take care of her.

Dallas was faultlessly thoughtful and considerate of her—something that could never have been said of Leo. And Dallas hadn't given the impression that he expected her, or anyone else, to put anything on hold or on the back burner for him. He'd even embraced her having this baby despite the fact that, early on, he'd clearly been confused by why she was doing it this way.

Never once had she felt taken advantage of, the way she had with Leo, and not until Dallas's request that she and Noelle move into his house had she felt as if she had to do more compromising than Dallas had done or was willing to do.

Yes, to be with him would mean uprooting herself. It would mean taking Noelle home to his house rather than to her apartment. But that wasn't because he was set in his ways or because he used that as an excuse to control what went on. It was just the best, most logical way for things to work out.

And other than that, she thought that Dallas was right that having kids made being set in his ways impossible. And he was okay with that. He was even okay with adding her baby to his family. And having more...

More that could come out of nights like the one they'd spent together. The night that had left her wanting nothing so much as to be back in his arms.

"Are you even listening to me?" her mother asked.

She wasn't.

But now that her mother had forced her to, Nina knew that even if she was willing to move into Dallas's house and life, even if she was willing to be a replacement mother to his boys and give her new daughter three big brothers, there was still the issue of the animosity between his family and hers.

Especially the obviously flaming animosity her family held on to, even if his had backed away from the feud enough to allow her in....

"Please don't, Mom," Nina said in a quiet voice when her mother had gone on to disparage Dallas and the rest of the Traubs. "I love that man. Please don't make me choose—"

"Choose!" her mother repeated as if the possibility of that hadn't occurred to her. "Are you telling me that you would pick *him* over us? *Them* over us?"

"I don't want to pick anyone over anyone. And I don't think I should have to. Especially when you can't tell me—right here and now, without any question—why you hate the Traubs. And don't bring up the election because Nate's gone on just fine not being mayor and can run again if he wants to. Even against a Traub if it was done less mean-spiritedly, which it could be."

"I can't believe what I'm hearing."

"The Traubs are just like us, Mom," Nina went on. "They're a family who care about each other. And about Rust Creek Falls. Just like us. They're making their way through life the same way we are. There's no reason, no sense in hating them because somebody got mad at somebody a gazillion years ago."

"You wouldn't really turn your back on us? Take that baby away from us…?" Laura Crawford asked in a whisper full of disbelief, obviously not in agreement with anything Nina had said but beginning to fear she might actually lose her daughter or her new—and first—grandchild.

"No, I wouldn't turn my back on you or take Noelle away from you. But I want to be with Dallas." And as Nina said that, she knew just how true it was. True enough to weather whatever conflicts arose from joining the two families because she suddenly couldn't see her life without him. She couldn't see herself raising Noelle without him. She couldn't see anything without him.

"And if I'm with Dallas, then it's up to you," she continued, thinking to illustrate what that would mean for her mother, should her family opt to go on the way they had been. "Will you not come to Noelle's christening or her birthday parties because the Traubs do? Will you only see Noelle when I can bring her to you because you won't visit her and see Dallas or his boys? Will you keep us at arm's length just for some fight that took place generations before any of us were even born?"

"So what is it you see, Nina?" her mother demanded angrily. "The Traubs and the Crawfords just getting together and hugging and kissing and pretending we haven't hated each other for decades? Becoming bosom buddies?"

Sadly, no, she didn't see that.

But Nina refused to just bow to the status quo.

"At first they were only civil to me," Nina informed her mother, outlining the course of her own path to the Traubs. "Then things became a little more friendly because they were glad that Dallas was happier when he was with me—the way I feel when I'm with him," she said pointedly. "And when they found out I was going to be alone on Christmas they invited me to join them. The same way you've invited more people than I can count to join us whenever you've heard of anyone we know spending a holiday alone. No, there hasn't been any hugging and kissing—" *well, with Traubs other than Dallas, anyway* "—but they opened their door to me, they were nice and hospitable, and it's gotten easier as it's gone along."

"So put a good face on it, is that what you're saying? And pretend we haven't been at each other's throats forever?"

"Yes," Nina said. "Start that way. For my sake. For *Noelle's* sake. Do what Dallas asked—just put the stupid rift behind us and try something else."

Laura Crawford was still frowning over that surgical mask but her tone was more resigned when she said, "You're serious about this? About this man? Isn't he as old as Leo?"

Ah, an attempt to throw a wrench into the works, because her mother knew Nina's thinking about that...

"Yes, he's almost as old as Leo, but he's a completely different person," Nina said, knowing that as a fact, pure and simple, and not daunted at all anymore by their age difference.

"And three kids, Nina," her mother said, trying again. "He already has *three* kids."

"Three kids who need a mom. Three kids who I already love and want to be a mom to."

"And you'd leave your little apartment

and let yourself be swallowed up in his life. Isn't that what you did with Leo? What you weren't going to do again?"

"I'd leave my apartment to live in a nice house, but it isn't the same as what I had to do with Leo because nothing is the same with Dallas. He left his kids, his family on *Christmas* to do what needed to be done for me because he takes care of what needs to be taken care of. Like I do. He goes with the flow— that makes him the exact opposite of Leo."

"But they're Traubs…" her mother said, sounding defeated.

"They're just people. A family. The same as we are."

"I don't know how this will work," her mother lamented.

"I think that if you try, and they try, eventually it can."

Her mother rolled her eyes, shook her head, frowned mightily. And yet there was still some semblance of acceptance. Unwilling and resentful, but acceptance on some level. "And I thought artificial insemination and having a baby without a husband was over-the-top enough. Leave it to you to add Traubs to the mix," she grumbled.

But, for now, that was concession enough

for Nina, and she realized that she just had to have faith that something better would come later, that even if both families began by just going through the motions of peace, eventually maybe peace would become a reality and grow into something better. Something that could genuinely put behind them whatever it was that had kept them at odds.

Her mother had just taken her hand to squeeze and leaned over to place a kiss to her forehead through the surgical mask when Dallas knocked on the door, tentatively poking just his head into the room.

"I thought you might want to know, Mrs. Crawford—they're about to change Noelle's diaper. If you want, they'll do it at the nursery window so you can see all ten fingers and all ten toes, and that she really is just perfect."

And maybe what the two families could be brought together for.

"I need to go see that," Laura Crawford said, tearing up again at the mere thought of the baby.

"Go," Nina encouraged her.

She watched as her mother returned to the door and stopped in front of Dallas, where he'd remained just to the outside of it.

For a moment Laura Crawford didn't speak,

she merely stood there, proudly, stubbornly. But then she straightened her shoulders and raised her chin to the big man and said, "Thank you for taking care of my daughter and my granddaughter."

It was slightly begrudging, only coolly courteous, but an improvement nonetheless.

"You're welcome. It was my pleasure," Dallas answered with more warmth.

Then Nina's mother went past him and down the corridor, and Dallas came back to sit on the side of Nina's bed.

He took her hand in both of his, raised it to kiss and when he'd tucked it against his thigh, he said, "Poor Noelle has to have a diaper change whether she needs it or not because there's one more thing I have to say, and I had to get back here to say it."

Nina smiled at him. "You said quite a bit before."

"But there's one more thing—if it isn't too late…" He glanced over his shoulder at the door to see if the coast was still clear. Then, looking at her again, his blue eyes delving into hers, he said, "I love you, Nina, and I'd really, really—*really*—like it if you'd say yes, you'll marry me…"

Nina teared up herself for the umpteenth time, smiled and didn't even need another moment to think about it before she said, "Yes, I will marry you."

A shocked sort of happiness infused Dallas's expression. "You will?"

Nina laughed. "My mother had a lot to say and it gave me a while to think when I was supposed to be listening," she confided, going on to tell him how she'd resolved her own issues and the realizations she'd come to about him, about everything.

"I love you, too," she told him. "I don't know how it happened when I was trying to make sure it didn't, but it did…"

"I know, I was fighting it, too. It was just bigger and stronger than I am."

And that was saying something.

"But what about your mom and the rest of your family?" Dallas asked, nodding in the direction of the hospital room door.

"I told her how I feel about you. That I want to be with you. So seeing her granddaughter might be more limited if she and everyone else keeps up the way they have been. And she doesn't want that. So I'm hoping that she and everyone else will come around."

"That's why she was nicer a minute ago?"

Nina laughed. "Well, yes, that's why she's trying. If everybody just tries—"

"We'll make it work out," Dallas assured her, reaching a hand to the back of her neck as he leaned forward to kiss her. Deeply, profoundly, oh-so-sweetly and yet with passion right there, too...

And that was what Nina really needed. The touch of Dallas's hands. The heat and strength of his body. The feel of his mouth pressed to hers. And that connection that had formed between them despite every obstacle and issue that should have prevented it.

She truly loved this man and wanted to spend the rest of her life with him.

When the kiss ended and she looked more closely at him, she saw the fatigue lurking behind his eyes and knew he needed some rest.

"Go home and sleep," she urged in a quiet voice filled with her own reluctance to lose his company.

"I'd rather round up some of my brothers and start to move you and Noelle to my place," he said, more question than statement. "Are you gonna let me do that?"

Nina smiled. "I don't think you and three boys will fit into my apartment, so yes, you can do that." Because even though she'd been looking forward to bringing her new baby home to the bright yellow nursery she'd decorated, the thought of going anywhere Dallas wasn't didn't appeal to her. "But you must know better than anyone that that means you're signing on for sleepless nights."

He smiled back at her. "Consider me signed on."

"But get some rest before you start moving day," she decreed.

"A couple of hours," he agreed. "A couple more to move things. Then I'll be back."

She already couldn't wait.

But he still didn't seem eager to leave because he stayed there, studying her awhile longer, kissing her again, telling her how much he loved her.

And only when Nina reminded him that her mother would be back any minute, and told him it was probably better if she was alone with her to tell her they were engaged, did he give Nina one last, lingering kiss, and actually go.

But not without leaning in first and whispering, "We're going to have a great life together…"

And leaving Nina certain that they would.

Epilogue

"Welcome, everyone, to the grand reopening of our elementary school, and thank you for coming out before you get your New Year's Eve parties started!" Mayor Collin Traub said over the microphone.

He was standing at a podium set up in the school cafeteria in front of a hundred occupied folding chairs while the rest of the audience filled the perimeters of the room because there weren't enough seats.

Nina was sitting in the center of the third row. It was Noelle's first outing and the newborn was sleeping peacefully beside her in

Dallas's arms—which had become Noelle's favorite place to snooze.

To Nina's left were her parents and those of her siblings who could make the event, and to Dallas's right was his family, with Ryder, Jake and Robbie interspersed between uncles.

During the week since Nina and Noelle had left the hospital and moved in with Dallas and the boys, the Crawfords and the Traubs had crossed paths and reached an unspoken truce of sorts. At first, barely civil hellos had been the only exchanges. As the week progressed, "How are you?" had been added on both sides. And with most of their focus on Noelle, Ryder, Jake and Robbie, so far the two families seemed to be tolerating each other.

It wasn't great, but it was something.

And having them all in that room at that moment, sitting in the same row of chairs, was enough to have caused a buzz throughout the cafeteria when townsfolk began to notice that a détente between the families had been reached.

"The flood cost us dearly." Rust Creek's new mayor began what sounded like a prepared speech. "Including the life of our former mayor, Hunter McGee, and I'd like us to spend a moment in silent remembrance."

That request was honored by everyone except a few fussy babies and very small children.

When the moment had been observed, Collin picked up where he'd left off.

"As you can see, thanks to the involvement of the New York organization Bootstraps, and the volunteers who came to Rust Creek Falls, the mission to bring our school back from the flood damage and make it better than ever has been accomplished. We want to thank everyone for their efforts and generosity of time and energy."

Applause and cheers went up.

When it died down, Collin said, "We want to particularly thank Lissa Roarke, who brought our situation to the attention of the whole country and whose television appearance and writings on our behalf have generated donations and help and—" the mayor smiled "—the interest—I hear—of any number of single women who just might like to find a Rust Creek cowboy of their own. Like my brother Braden, for instance, who is now the only one of us left single."

The crowd laughed at the brotherly goad.

"Sorry, Braden," Collin apologized remorselessly. "But I wanted a lead into making some announcements and congratulations, and your status as an available bachelor got to be it."

More chuckles from the audience.

"While we aren't all out from under the destruction the flood left," Collin said, "I think we should note that from the bad came some good. And as this New Year is upon us, I want to take the time to recognize and celebrate that good the same way we're here celebrating our resurrected and improved school."

There were mutterings of agreement to that.

"I know you're all looking at that third row, there," Collin went on, "where the Crawfords and the Traubs are actually sitting together. If you'll notice, my brother Dallas and Nina Crawford—and Nina's not-quite-a-week-old daughter, Noelle—are right there in the middle, and that says it all because they're the connecting link. Seems like Christmas brought them together and—in keeping with the holiday theme—Dallas and Nina are engaged and have set a Valentine's Day wedding date."

More clapping and cheers of congratulations rang through the room. Nina wasn't sure how much of it might be for the ending of the feud between the two families, but she knew that some of it was for her and Dallas. So she smiled and glanced at Dallas, who smiled back, leaned over and kissed her.

"But they're not the only two pairing up," Mayor Traub went on. "As you all know, your kindergarten teacher, Willa Christensen, and I came together over the flood and ended up tying the knot, and so did Dean Pritchett and Shelby Jenkins, and our newest addition to veterinary medicine—Brooks Smith and Jazzy Cates.

"And not only did we come out with three weddings, but Gage Christensen has the flood to thank for bringing him Lissa," the young mayor continued. "And my brother Sutter and our fifth-grade teacher, Paige Dalton, have reunited after five years, and just announced to us that they'll be having a January wedding—so that makes three engagements, too."

Collin winked at Sutter and Paige, who had also told the family that Paige was pregnant—although they didn't think it was good for her image as a schoolteacher to let that news get around until after the wedding.

"The efforts to help Rust Creek Falls survive and come back better than ever have brought out the best in us all, I think," Collin said. "It's even offered an opportunity for redemption for some—particularly for Arthur Swinton."

Nina saw the reservations that name raised in the crowd that was clearly unsure what was to come, since the Thunder Canyon former city councilman and mayor had taken such a big fall from grace in the past few years.

"Due to the persistence of Arthur's newfound son, Shane Roarke, and Shane's adopted family, Arthur's sentence has been commuted and he's been released from jail."

There were mutterings about that that weren't all favorable.

But before they got out of hand, Collin said, "I know some of you won't agree with that, but Arthur has vowed to devote the rest of his life to positive change and I, for one, wish him the best in that pursuit. Arthur has set about proving his intentions by raising—legally—a large sum of money that he's donating to our town renovation project to ensure that Rust Creek Falls continues to rebuild and grow!"

Collin's victorious tone was answered with more applause, though even that held some reserve.

When it died down once more, Collin concluded his speech, reminding them all of a few humorous moments during the past year, sending out some tongue-in-cheek congratulations and lightening the tone from there.

Then he said, "That's about it for me tonight. But DJ's Rib Shack, owned by my cousin DJ Traub in Thunder Canyon, has provided us with a full meal to mark this occasion. We'll be setting up for that while you all tour the school, and when you get back here dinner'll be served."

Enthusiasm for that was unmistakable.

"And just let me be the first to wish us all a Happy New Year!" Collin concluded.

"Happy New Year!" the crowd echoed as everyone stood to take the school tour.

A beautiful job had been done restoring, rejuvenating and restocking the building, and that was all pointed out by the principal, who gave the tour.

Along the way, Robbie took the hand of Laura Crawford—whom he'd developed a fondness for—on one side, and his own grandmother on the other. Nina saw it and couldn't help smiling at how both women put aside their differences to indulge the little boy—a sign of the future, she hoped.

By the time everyone returned to the school

cafeteria it had been transformed back into just that, with bench-lined tables all set out and the kitchen open and ready to serve the delicious meal that was one of several gifts the Thunder Canyon branch of the Traub family had sent to help its neighbors during these long months of struggle.

And as Nina sat with Dallas by her side, who was still cradling Noelle in one arm while keeping his other arm around her, she felt such a sense of happiness and contentment come over her that it made her well up.

Rust Creek Falls would survive and go on providing the home she'd always known, the home she never wanted to leave. And now, not only did she have the child she'd wanted and been denied for too long, but she had Dallas and Ryder and Jake and Robbie—an entire family—to share it with.

"What are you thinking about, Miss-Nina-with-the-tears-in-her-eyes?" Dallas asked, leaning close to her ear so that she alone could hear him, he alone noticing that she was in the throes of emotions.

"I was just thinking how much I love you," she said. "And Noelle and the boys, and this whole town. And how glad I am to spend the rest of my life here with you."

Dallas pressed a warm kiss to her cheek and stayed there a long moment before he nuzzled her ear with his nose and whispered, "If anyone had told me a year ago that I'd be where I am now, I'd have called them a liar. But the truth is, you've made me the luckiest man on earth."

Nina could only smile at that and turn to kiss him, knowing that luck had shone down on them both through the blinding blizzard and opened their eyes to what was right there waiting for them in each other.

* * * * *

Get 4 FREE REWARDS!

We'll send you 2 FREE Books plus 2 FREE Mystery Gifts.

FREE Value Over **$20**

Both the **Harlequin® Historical** and **Harlequin® Romance** series feature compelling novels filled with emotion and simmering romance.

YES! Please send me 2 FREE novels from the Harlequin Historical or Harlequin Romance series and my 2 FREE gifts (gifts are worth about $10 retail). After receiving them, if I don't wish to receive any more books, I can return the shipping statement marked "cancel." If I don't cancel, I will receive 6 brand-new Harlequin Historical books every month and be billed just $5.94 each in the U.S. or $6.49 each in Canada, a savings of at least 12% off the cover price or 4 brand-new Harlequin Romance Larger-Print every month and be billed just $5.84 each in the U.S. or $5.99 each in Canada, a savings of at least 14% off the cover price. It's quite a bargain! Shipping and handling is just 50¢ per book in the U.S. and $1.25 per book in Canada.* I understand that accepting the 2 free books and gifts places me under no obligation to buy anything. I can always return a shipment and cancel at any time by calling the number below. The free books and gifts are mine to keep no matter what I decide.

Choose one: ☐ **Harlequin Historical** ☐ **Harlequin Romance Larger-Print**
(246/349 HDN GRAE)   (119/319 HDN GRAQ)

Name (please print)

Address   Apt. #

City   State/Province   Zip/Postal Code

Email: Please check this box ☐ if you would like to receive newsletters and promotional emails from Harlequin Enterprises ULC and its affiliates. You can unsubscribe anytime.

> **Mail to the Harlequin Reader Service:**
> **IN U.S.A.:** P.O. Box 1341, Buffalo, NY 14240-8531
> **IN CANADA:** P.O. Box 603, Fort Erie, Ontario L2A 5X3

Want to try 2 free books from another series! Call 1-800-873-8635 or visit www.ReaderService.com.

*Terms and prices subject to change without notice. Prices do not include sales taxes, which will be charged (if applicable) based on your state or country of residence. Canadian residents will be charged applicable taxes. Offer not valid in Quebec. This offer is limited to one order per household. Books received may not be as shown. Not valid for current subscribers to the Harlequin Historical or Harlequin Romance series. All orders subject to approval. Credit or debit balances in a customer's account(s) may be offset by any other outstanding balance owed by or to the customer. Please allow 4 to 6 weeks for delivery. Offer available while quantities last.

Your Privacy—Your information is being collected by Harlequin Enterprises ULC, operating as Harlequin Reader Service. For a complete summary of the information we collect, how we use this information and to whom it is disclosed, please visit our privacy notice located at corporate.harlequin.com/privacy-notice. From time to time we may also exchange your personal information with reputable third parties. If you wish to opt out of this sharing of your personal information, please visit readerservice.com/consumerschoice or call 1-800-873-8635. **Notice to California Residents**—Under California law, you have specific rights to control and access your data. For more information on these rights and how to exercise them, visit corporate.harlequin.com/california-privacy.

HHHRLP22R2

Get 4 FREE REWARDS!

We'll send you 2 FREE Books plus 2 FREE Mystery Gifts.

FREE
Value Over
$20

Both the **Harlequin Intrigue®** and **Harlequin® Romantic Suspense** series feature compelling novels filled with heart-racing action-packed romance that will keep you on the edge of your seat.

YES! Please send me 2 FREE novels from the Harlequin Intrigue or Harlequin Romantic Suspense series and my 2 FREE gifts (gifts are worth about $10 retail). After receiving them, if I don't wish to receive any more books, I can return the shipping statement marked "cancel." If I don't cancel, I will receive 6 brand-new Harlequin Intrigue Larger-Print books every month and be billed just $6.24 each in the U.S. or $6.74 each in Canada, a savings of at least 14% off the cover price or 4 brand-new Harlequin Romantic Suspense books every month and be billed just $5.24 each in the U.S. or $5.99 each in Canada, a savings of at least 13% off the cover price. It's quite a bargain! Shipping and handling is just 50¢ per book in the U.S. and $1.25 per book in Canada.* I understand that accepting the 2 free books and gifts places me under no obligation to buy anything. I can always return a shipment and cancel at any time by calling the number below. The free books and gifts are mine to keep no matter what I decide.

Choose one: ☐ **Harlequin Intrigue**
Larger-Print
(199/399 HDN GRA2)

☐ **Harlequin Romantic Suspense**
(240/340 HDN GRCE)

Name (please print)

Address   Apt. #

City   State/Province   Zip/Postal Code

Email: Please check this box ☐ if you would like to receive newsletters and promotional emails from Harlequin Enterprises ULC and its affiliates. You can unsubscribe anytime.

Mail to the **Harlequin Reader Service:**
IN U.S.A.: P.O. Box 1341, Buffalo, NY 14240-8531
IN CANADA: P.O. Box 603, Fort Erie, Ontario L2A 5X3

Want to try 2 free books from another series! Call 1-800-873-8635 or visit www.ReaderService.com.

HIHRS22R2

HARLEQUIN
PLUS

Announcing a **BRAND-NEW** multimedia subscription service for romance fans like you!

Read, Watch and Play.

Experience the easiest way to get the romance content you crave.

Start your **FREE 7 DAY TRIAL** at
<u>www.harlequinplus.com/freetrial</u>.